Powerful, Loyal, Unforgettable

Follow the Titans

as they find true love

The Tycoon's Proposal

The Titan Series

Book Three

The Tycoon's Proposal

The Titans

Book Three

By

Melody Anne

Dedication

This book is dedicated to my favorite aunt, Janet.
I love you so much.
Thank you for making my childhood full of adventures, magic and fun.

NOTE FROM THE AUTHOR

So many times in life, we ask ourselves, "What if?" How would my life have turned out if I'd gone left instead of right? How many lives would be changed had I chosen a different fork in the road? I truly believe that if you're meant to be with someone, it will eventually work out. That's why I love to write romance and why all my stories must have a "happily ever after." Is it predictable? Certainly!! But the routes along the way to the end can make the adventure worth taking.

Thank you to all of you who read these books and find a place in your lives for the Titans and the Andersons. I love these families and hope you do, as well. The Titans are tough as nails and think they're in charge, but we all know it's the women who really have all the control. I'm saying this with an evil laugh, of course.

Thank you to all the people who help me along the way to complete these books. Thank you to my family, for whom all of this is done. Thank you to my fans, who are always so supportive. I hope you enjoy *The Tycoon's Proposal.*

With Love,
Melody Anne

PROLOGUE

Ryan Titan looked around his empty home with satisfaction. He'd watched his two cousins settle down over the last couple of years, going from Seattle's most eligible bachelors to happily married men, and now he was left feeling like he was missing something.

His cousins, Derek and Drew, were far more like brothers to him than cousins. They'd been raised next to each other and had all gone from poverty level to billionaire status together. They'd each done separate things in the business world but stayed by each other's sides as they climbed to the top of the world's richest ranks.

Ryan felt a bit excluded as he watched his cousins find their true loves, leaving him behind for once. He was always welcome in their homes, but now it was different. He was actually filled with envy as he watched them with their families.

There he stood in a new house without furniture. He shook his head as he wandered around the rooms, his steps echoing off the bare walls. He heard a knock at the door and heard it opening.

"Ryan, where are you?"

"I'm coming," he called back, as he heard the voice of his nephew. Jacob rounded the corner, and the breath was pushed out of Ryan's body, as his thirteen-year-old "nephew" hurled himself into his arms.

"This place is great, Uncle Ryan," Jacob said with enthusiasm. He raced off to check out the home. Ryan was glad he'd bought a place so close to his cousins because Jacob and the rest of his "nieces" and "nephews" could come over anytime.

"Nice place, Ryan," Derek said as he joined them.

"I'm lucky to have found a place so close to you and Drew. I already mapped out the backyard, and we can make a trail between the properties. Then the kids can ride four-wheelers back and forth. We can make a killer trail for all of us," Ryan said. He was excited to get started on the project. There would be no need for fences between the properties.

"Great thinking, cousin. You map it all out, and I'll get the people in to forge the trail," Derek replied.

"Hey, maybe I don't want to tear up my yard. What if I want to keep you hooligans out?" Drew entered the room and jumped into the conversation. Both cousins ignored him, knowing he didn't mean a word of it.

"Where are the ladies?" Ryan asked. He'd expected them to be right behind their husbands.

"They're taking a spa day today. The young ones are at my house," Derek answered.

"They're already spectacular and in no way need to go to the spa," Ryan told them. Both cousins nodded, as they worshiped their wives. However, they would go to the ends of the earth for them and give them absolutely anything they wanted.

"When are you going to finally settle down?" Derek asked him.

"You know me. I don't want a lady coming into my life and messing with a good thing," Ryan said. His typical arrogant smile was on his face, but there was no real meaning behind his words. He was thinking that being single wasn't as great as it had once been. As he looked around at his empty home, he thought it would be pretty great to share it with someone.

He shook off his melancholy mood and showed his cousins around. Unbelievably, the home was even larger than his two cousins' homes. He hadn't planned on the huge place, but the location was what sold him. He wanted to be near his cousins. The older he got, the more he wanted to slow down a bit.

Ryan was a phenomenal architect and remodeled historic homes, which was a hobby for him and not his main career. He'd made his first

9

million in the stock market and his first billion through his many business investments. He had more money than he could ever spend in a lifetime and, although he spent a lot of time in the office still, he took off when he wanted to so he could pursue his love of historic properties.

Ryan called his secretary and gave her free rein on getting his house furnished. Then he headed to the backyard with his cousins so they could plan the quad trail. The rest of the day flew by, and Ryan forgot all about his troubles.

CHAPTER ONE

Nicole Lander parked her car, saying a prayer of thanks that it had once again made it home. She was grateful each time she turned the key and the engine decided to turn over and work for another day.

She climbed the broken staircase, careful to not lean against the rusted out railing. She'd made that mistake once and had almost fallen through. The only thing that saved her had been her great reflexes.

11

She reached her door, inserted the key, and spent the next couple of minutes wiggling it around until it finally grasped the mechanisms inside the knob and turned. She rushed inside, quickly relocking the door. She breathed a sigh of relief as she entered the safety of her apartment. She'd seriously be in trouble if someone was ever chasing her because she certainly wouldn't be able to get inside quickly enough to save herself.

Nicole looked around the worn out studio apartment in disgust. It was sparsely furnished with secondhand furniture which had seen much better days. She tried to make her place as homey as possible, but with her very limited budget, there wasn't very much she could do. She opened her refrigerator, only to spot the empty shelves and shut it back up. She was exhausted and only had a few hours to sleep before she had to report to her temporary job.

She was so exhausted she could barely stand on her feet. She was working about twenty hours a day, six days a week, plus a few hours on her seventh day. She couldn't wait until she found a permanent, full-time job so she could actually have some decent hours. Between her jobs and visiting with her sister in the hospital, she knew she looked like a complete wreck.

She fell face first on her bed and wasn't happy when her telephone woke her up a short hour later. She crawled from the bed to pick it up because she knew it had to be important."Hello," she croaked into the phone.

"We're looking for Nicole Lander," said the voice on the other end of the line.

"This is Nicole. How can I help you?" She replied, a bit more awake.

"We've pre-screened you for a full-time job and think you'd be perfect for the position," the woman said.

Nicole was on instant alert. "I'd love to hear about it," she told the woman.

"The position is for a live-in housekeeper. You'd be provided room and board, plus a generous salary if you're interested in coming in for an interview."

"I'll be there whenever you need me to be," Nicole said, without needing to ask any questions. She didn't care if she scrubbed toilets all day, as long as she could get out of her current flat. "When do you want me?"

"You need to come into the office and fill out some paperwork. Confidentiality is a must while working for this client. You'll have to sign papers attesting to the fact that you won't speak about what happens in the household. You'll also be required to submit to a drug test. Your background check is already complete. If you come into the office this afternoon, we can interview you. I want to let you know there are a few other people interested."

"I'll be down there in a half hour. I have no problem signing whatever you need," Nicole told her. She hoped she wasn't sounding too desperate.

"That sounds great, Nicole. I'll be waiting for you," she said before disconnecting the call. Nicole thought the client must be one of those wealthy hermits who didn't like the world to see them. She really didn't care. Her temp company wouldn't send her to an unsafe place. Even if her room was tiny, it would be better than the studio in which she currently resided. She was on the verge of losing the place, anyway, because her sister's hospital bills were depleting her bank account.

Even though she hadn't gotten enough sleep, she was wired with excitement running through her veins. She jumped into the shower and made it to the offices in just under thirty minutes. She walked from the interview, confident she'd be selected. By the time she got back home and crawled into bed, sleep overtook her and she felt some peace, which she hadn't felt in far too long.

When she got the call the next day, she hung her head and barely managed to hold the tears back. Someone else had gotten the position. She was running out of options. She didn't know how she was going to take care of Patsy's hospital bills and still keep a roof over their heads. She got dressed and headed toward her waitressing job, where she'd be lucky to take home thirty dollars in tips for a ten-hour shift. It wasn't much motivation, but it was better than nothing.

###

Three months later, Nicole sat by her phone, trying to work up her courage. She had to call him. There was no other choice. Nicole was cringing at the thought of groveling at Ryan Titan's feet, but she really didn't see any other options. Her sister needed the operation and, as hard as Nicole worked, she still couldn't pay for it. The hospital didn't care if it was a life or death matter. They only cared about the bottom line. She couldn't believe they said it was an elective surgery. It was something slowly killing her, though — not an emergency. They wouldn't perform it without payment in full.

Nicole took a deep breath, her hand resting on the phone. She'd been in the same position for the last hour, trying to force herself to pick it up. Her palms were sweaty, and her heart was beating irregularly — out of control. The tear tracks down her cheeks had long since dried, but the terror was still there.

She hadn't talked to Ryan in twelve years, and their last conversation hadn't gone well. He still believed she'd cheated on him. It had been so much easier to let him believe that, but oh how it had broken her heart.

She told herself repeatedly it wasn't about her. It was about her little sister, and no matter how much he may hate her, he'd always loved Patsy. There was no way he'd sit back and let her die when he could help her.

She wiped her hands on her jeans and picked up the handle of the phone, trying to control her trembling hands. She had to redial the number three times. She was shaking so hard she kept punching the wrong numbers.

As the phone started to ring, her nerves reached the breaking point. She was hoping it would go to voicemail. Then she could just leave a message and not have to face hearing his voice.

"Who is this?" a voice demanded, startling her.

"Th . . . this is Nicole," she stuttered. There was an uncomfortably long pause on the other end of the line.

"Nicole who?" came the same voice, as cool as ice.

"Nicole Lander," she said, barely above a whisper.

"How did you get my personal number?" he demanded. She was thinking she'd made a really bad mistake. It sounded as if he didn't even remember who she was. Maybe their time together had been far more significant to her than it had been to him.

"I got it from your uncle," she finally managed to say. There was another really long silence at her words.

"What do you want?" he demanded.

"I . . . um . . . wanted to see if I could . . . um . . . talk to you about something important," she forced through her trembling lips. "We used to know each other a really long time ago. I don't know if you still remember me," she finished.

"I don't have time to beat around the bush. Spit out what it is you want," he demanded of her. She didn't want to ask him for money over the phone, but what choice did she have?

"My little sister is in the hospital. She needs an operation, and we don't have any other options. Your uncle said I should talk to you," she finally pushed out, on the verge of crying once again. She could tell by his tone of voice he was simply humoring her and, in no way, was he going to help them out. Nicole was going to lose her baby sister, and she didn't think she could possibly make it through the horrific experience.

He was silent for so long she thought he'd hung up the phone. Ryan didn't remember Nicole or her sister, and he was far too important a man to sit there on the phone with her. She'd failed her last resort and she felt an overwhelming sense of grief. She was starting to take the phone from her ear when he finally spoke again.

"Do you know where my office is?"

"Yes, in the city," she mumbled.

"Be there tomorrow at five," he said, and then she heard nothing but a dial tone.

Nicole sat there for a couple of minutes, in shock, as the phone continued to beep at her. She finally managed to hang up and allowed the tears to fall down her cheeks. It wasn't hopeless. Ryan was willing to hear her out. She didn't care what it took. Nicole had to convince him to help her baby sister. She couldn't lose her.

###

Ryan sat at his desk, feeling a myriad of emotions coursing through him. He'd known who was on the other end of his line from the very first word she'd whispered. He could never forget that voice. It had haunted his dreams for the past twelve years. She'd been the girl who got away. Hell, not only got away, but thrust him from her life.

He ran his hands through his hair and let out a sigh of frustration. How he wished he could've simply told her to go to hell and hung up the phone, but there was no way he could be that much of a bastard. He'd loved Patsy as if she was his own little sister.

He felt a smile lift the corner of his lips, as he thought back to little Patsy toddling around his legs as he spent time with Nicole. She had become attached to him from the very first moment he came through her doors. Over the years he'd watched her grow up, she'd squeezed a piece of his heart.

Ryan hadn't heard Patsy was hurt. He decided to make some calls and get some background information on the situation. He needed to be well prepared when Nicole stepped through his doors. He'd been incredibly surprised by her call. He wasn't having any more surprises when she stepped back into his life. He also needed to speak to his uncle. He didn't know what the old man was up to, but he knew not to give his number out to anyone. His uncle should've taken her number and given it to Ryan. That way he wouldn't have been surprised. He didn't like to be blindsided.

By the time Ryan got the answers he was looking for, he hung his head in shame. He couldn't believe how bad things had gotten for Patsy. He knew beyond any shadow of a doubt he'd help her, but Nicole didn't know that. He'd help Patsy, but he was also going to get what he wanted from Nicole.

She'd once thought he wasn't good enough for her, and now he was the only one who could save her baby sister. He felt a sense of justice in that knowledge. He knew there wasn't any point in working the rest of the day, as he couldn't concentrate. He was eager for his appointment the next day. A smile stole across his features as he sat back in his chair. He enjoyed a challenge, and Nicole would definitely provide him some entertainment.

He made several phone calls, which included getting Patsy moved to a private room. He then found the best Cardiothoracic surgeon he could find and called him in for a consult. Ryan didn't do anything in half-measures, and he wanted to make sure Patsy received only the best of care.

By the time he hung up the phone, he felt more in control. Patsy was going to be well taken care of, and he was going to get his chance for redemption with Nicole. She'd pay for what she'd done to him, and they'd both enjoy the punishment.

Ryan headed home, feeling better than he had felt in a long while. That somewhat empty feeling he had been dealing with for quite some time seemed to have completely lifted. He found himself smiling as he jogged up the stairs to change clothing. He was meeting up with Drew later in the evening and decided to enjoy his great mood.

Nicole paced outside the high rise building, working up her courage to enter through the double doors. He wouldn't have told her to come in unless he was going to help her sister. He may hate her for what he thought she'd done to him, but he used to be the kindest person she knew, and there was no way he could let Patsy die.

She squared her shoulders and held her head up high as she entered the plush interior of Titan Enterprises. Even the lobby of the building screamed luxury, with its marble floors and huge security desk. There were plants strategically placed to make the area warm and inviting, and several people were moving around the lobby, coming in and out of different doors. Nicole didn't know if the room was supposed to seem intimidating or not, but it certainly made her feel out of place. The people he dealt with on a daily basis most likely didn't notice the luxury surrounding them, as they were around it all the time.

The guard behind the desk looked pleasant enough, but Nicole could see the steel in his gaze. If she wasn't on the acceptable list, there was no way she'd make it to the elevators. She had to fight every instinct in her, which told her to turn around and run away. She was made stronger than that and wouldn't back down. She'd fought harder battles in her life, but her sister's surgery was the only one she'd ever fought with her whole being.

She tried to walk with as much confidence as she could muster. What if having her come in had been nothing but a cruel joke, and the guard was going to send her on her way? If that was the case, she'd leave kicking and screaming. There was nothing she wouldn't do for her sister, even if it meant humiliating herself.

"Do you have an appointment?" the man asked.

"Yes, I'm here to see Mr. Titan," she answered. She'd been trying to sound confident, but her throaty voice sounded weak, even to her own ears. She took a few deep breaths, trying to pull herself together.

"Your name, please?" the guard asked.

"Nicole Lander." The man looked at his computer for a moment, and she had to quell the rising panic. After what seemed an inordinately long time, though it was only seconds, he nodded his head and handed her a badge.

"Go to the elevators and swipe this badge. Go up to the twentieth floor. When you step off the elevators, go to the right, and you'll find the reception desk. Mr. Titan is expecting you, so check in with his secretary," the man said. Nicole nodded at him to let him know she understood.

Walking over to the elevators, she pushed the button and waited. It felt like she was in a fog as the bell chimed and the doors opened. She stepped inside and had to fight her claustrophobia as the metal machine rose higher and higher. Instead of feeling comforted by the music, she felt more closed in. She hated small places. As the numbers lit up, signaling her imminent arrival, she could feel her breathing become shallower. She was seconds away from seeing her first love, and she had a feeling the meeting would be quite chilling.

She'd wanted him to hate her when she pushed him out of her life. It had been a far better option than the alternative. There was no way she wanted him to know who she really was. She'd much rather have him look at her with anger and contempt in his eyes than pity or disgust from knowing the truth.

The doors opened, and she jumped a bit when the bell signaled her arrival. On wooden legs, she stepped from the doors and made her way to the beautiful desk, which sat in the middle of a huge reception area.

"Name, please?" the woman asked, barely looking up from her computer.

"Nicole Lander," she answered in a voice that was a bit stronger than the one she'd used with the security guard. The woman picked up her phone and spoke into it for a moment.

"Mr. Titan is currently busy. He asked me to tell you to have a seat. He'll call you when he's finished up," the woman said. She turned back to her computer, confident Nicole would do what she was told.

Nicole walked over to one of the plush seats and picked up a magazine. She glanced at her watch every few minutes. She was anxious to get back. She really wanted to make it to the hospital to visit with her sister before she had to report in to her waitressing job.

The time continued to tick by, and she was seething mad once an hour had passed. She figured she'd be in his office for no more than a half hour, but if she didn't get in there soon she wouldn't be able to visit her sister. She stepped up to the desk, thinking he'd forgotten about her.

"I wanted to make sure Mr. Titan knew I was still here," she said to the receptionist. She knew she had a bit of bite to her tone, but it was rude to make someone wait this long. He must assume he was the only one who had a life. The secretary looked up, startled, like she couldn't possibly believe Nicole would dare to question her boss's intentions.

"Mr. Titan's a very busy man. You'll have to wait for him to call you in," the woman rudely replied. Nicole nodded and took her seat again. Another half hour passed, still with no word from Ryan, and she could no longer wait. She couldn't afford to be late to her job. It looked like he'd played her for a fool. He was most likely in his office, watching her fidget from some hidden camera and having a nice laugh to himself.

She slowly got up and headed off toward the elevator. She didn't approach the reception desk again. Why bother? She took the elevator back downstairs and returned the badge to the security guard. She held her head high as she exited the building. She was going to barely make it to work on time, so she wouldn't allow the tears — that were trying so hard to escape — to fall.

She felt like she had failed her baby sister. She really didn't see any other options of being able to pay the surgery bill. She'd already given up her tiny apartment. She was living on friends' couches and her sister's hospital room chair. She had sold everything of value she owned, and it still wasn't enough. Her car decided when it wanted to work, which was only about half the time. She wasn't a person to give up on anything, but she didn't see what more she could possibly do.

She rushed in the doors of the second rate, all-night truck stop where she waitressed and put her purse away. She made it out to the floor with a minute to spare. Her boss looked up with a glare and pointedly glanced at the clock. He then went back to his paper and ignored her. It was going to be a long night, as she hadn't gotten a decent night's sleep in forever. She was used to that and would deal with it like she did everything thrown her way.

###

Ryan hadn't expected the business call to take so long and was about to pull his hair out when he finally managed to get off the phone. He'd been planning on making Nicole wait for a while, just to make sure she squirmed in her seat a bit. He wasn't normally so rude, though, as to make someone wait two hours.

"You can send Ms. Lander in now," he said into his intercom.

There was a pause before his efficient secretary came back. "It looks as if she left," came the reply. Ryan didn't say anything else. He hung up and called the security desk asking if she'd left the building, only to find out she'd indeed left about a half hour earlier. She wasn't acting like someone who wanted a favor. If any other person had walked out before he was ready to speak with them he would've scrapped the whole thing, but this wasn't business. It was personal.

He made some phone calls and found out where she was. When he discovered where she was working, his bad mood deepened even further. He really shouldn't give a damn where she worked or what she did. She shouldn't matter to him in the least, but when he thought about her working overnight at that dive of a truck stop, his stomach clenched. He knew the kind of people who habituated a place like that in the wee hours of the morning, and it was certainly no place for a woman.

He gathered up his things and called his driver. It looked like he was dining out that night. He smiled to himself when he pictured her reaction to him entering the joint. Hell, when his car pulled up, he was sure there would be a bit of a stir. People like him simply didn't go to places like that. At least, people like he was nowadays. He would've been happy to go anywhere when he was a kid. That would've been a real treat.

It took the driver about forty minutes to navigate traffic and pull up in front of the diner. It was fairly busy, and he looked through the windows, spotting her almost immediately. She'd changed in the years since he'd seen her last, but not much.

Her young, sleek body had matured and now she had curves, though he couldn't see them well beneath the loose clothing and apron she was wearing. Her hair was still dark and hung low on her back in an unflattering braid, which looked like she had made it up in minutes.

As he stepped through the diner doors and quickly browsed, he could see the weariness in her movements. When she finally turned to see who'd walked in and caused a silence to fall over her customers, he felt a kick in his gut by the sheer exhaustion of her expression.

She'd always been so full of life, and now she looked drained, as if she bore the weight of the world on her shoulders. She approached him slowly, looking at him as if he was a dangerous animal ready to strike any moment. His lips turned up in a sardonic smile because he was a dangerous animal--far more deadly than any four-legged creatures she might ever encounter.

"Do you want a table?" she asked him suspiciously.

"That would be great," he responded overconfidently.

"What would you like to drink?" she asked through clenched teeth.

"I'll take a coffee," he replied. He'd determined within minutes of walking in that she'd be leaving with him. He knew exactly what he wanted as payment for helping her sister. He'd enjoy a bit of cat and mouse in the meantime. He knew he'd win, so he could be indulgent for a while.

"Here's the menu. I'll be right back with your coffee," she said and walked off. He enjoyed the sway of her hips, which were slightly thicker than they had been when they were teenagers. She'd definitely turned into a woman, and he couldn't wait to explore the new her. She was still stunning, even with the stress and exhaustion etched into her features.

She returned with the coffee, and he noticed the mirth in her eyes as he took his first sip and a grimace passed over his features. It was horrible, and he had the feeling she was enjoying his suffering. He controlled his face and took another long sip, just so he could wipe that smug look off her face. She looked as if she was trying to control her expression, but she couldn't hide the twinkle in her gorgeous brown eyes.

"Are you ready to place your order?"

"What are your specials?" he asked in a serious tone. He enjoyed watching her try and act nonchalant with him, though she wasn't doing nearly as great of a job as she thought she was.

"We have the chef's meatloaf special, and we serve breakfast all day," she said sweetly. He perused the menu, like he really cared what he ordered. Her foot started tapping impatiently as she continued to wait for him.

"Ms. Lander, can you please come over here?" Ryan heard her boss call. He noticed the twinge she couldn't stop from crossing her features.

"Yes, Mr. Archer," she said, with a long look at Ryan before she turned.

Ryan watched her walk over to where her boss was standing and strained his ears to hear their conversation.

"Could you please try and act more professional? That man showed up in a Jaguar, and you're tapping your toe in impatience. Do you want to keep your job?" Nicole's boss threatened.

"Of course, sir. I'm sorry about that," Ryan heard her say. Her voice was subdued.

Her boss dismissed her, and Nicole walked back over to Ryan, fury evident in her eyes.

"I'm sorry about making you wait. Have you decided yet?" she asked him.

"I'll take a turkey sandwich and the soup of the day," he responded. Ryan didn't like the way her boss had spoken to her, and it only solidified his decision she'd be leaving with him. She jotted down his order and quickly disappeared.

Nicole served him his food quickly, and he forced himself to choke some of it down while he continued to watch her. She never stopped running as she refilled coffee and took down orders. She kept his glass topped off, along with those of the other twenty or so customers. He almost came out of his seat when he saw some trucker get a little bit too friendly. Ryan had to admit he was impressed how she handled the man, letting him know she was unavailable, while still being polite.

Ryan gave up on eating the terrible food and sat back, drinking the muddy coffee. He'd been there for a couple of hours, and several of the customers cleared out, and yet she was still running around. Her boss snapped orders at her left and right, and Nicole still managed to keep a positive attitude. She had to be dead on her feet.

Ryan wasn't going to take much more. "We need to talk," he told her when she came to top off his mug again.

"I can't talk right now. I'm working," she told him, somewhat exasperated.

"Have you had a break yet tonight?"

She looked at him as if he was insane. She was lucky to get to run to the bathroom on any given night. "I'm the only waitress here. I don't have time to take a break," she finally said and turned to walk away.

He grabbed her wrist and pulled her into the booth next to him. She gasped in outrage at his high-handedness.

"Ms. Lander, you have customers waiting for you," her boss said, thinking she was slacking on the job.

She looked at Ryan in a panic. If he was trying to get her fired, he was doing an excellent job. "I'm sorry, sir. I tripped," she said as she struggled to get back up.

"Ms. Lander hasn't had a break the entire time I've been here, and I'd like to speak to her for a few minutes," Ryan said to the man, glaring over at him.

"I don't appreciate you telling me how to treat my employees, as it's none of your business." Nicole's boss puffed up in anger. "Get back to work, Ms. Lander," he snapped.

She once again struggled to get up, but Ryan still refused to let her go. You're going to get me fired," she said through gritted teeth. She was starting to get scared. He could see the vulnerability in her eyes. He was done with the place, and she was leaving with him, even if he had to throw her over his shoulder.

"We're leaving now," he said as he released her and stood up. He threw some bills on the table and grabbed his jacket. Nicole quickly fled from him, then went around the tables and refilled her customers' glasses. He stood by the counter and waited until she was done.

"I need to use the restroom. I'll be right back," Nicole told her boss and quickly disappeared. Ryan's rage increased when the man nodded tightly. He couldn't believe she needed to get permission to use the bathroom. It was ridiculous.

He spotted the cook, who looked like an understanding man.

He pulled a couple hundred from his pocket and approached the guy. "Can you please grab Nicole's things for me? She's leaving with me now, whether she wants to or not, and I think she'd rather have her possessions," Ryan said to the guy, who sized him up. "I won't harm her. Our families have been friends since childhood, and she'll no longer need this job," he assured the cook.

"She should've left here long ago. The boss treats her like crap," the cook said. He grabbed her belongings and set them on the counter, then stood waiting for Nicole to come out. She appeared quickly, since it seemed she wasn't allowed more than a couple of minutes, even to use the restroom.

"Nicole, do you know this guy?" the cook asked.

Her shoulders seemed to sag a bit as she tried to figure out how to answer that question. "We grew up together. Don't worry, Bubba, he's not trying to hurt me," she assured the cook. She had no clue she'd just given the cook permission to let

Ryan cart her out of the restaurant, or she would've never said that. Bubba smiled at Ryan and gave him the thumbs up.

"Right then, let's go," he told Nicole once again.

"Ryan, I already told you I'm not going anywhere with you. I don't get off until eight in the morning," she almost yelled at him. She then looked over at her boss, who was glaring at her. "If you really want to talk to me, I'll come to your offices in the morning."

Ryan didn't feel the need to talk anymore. He grabbed her things up, then grabbed her around the waist and tossed her over his shoulder and started walking toward the front door.

Nicole said nothing until they were almost to the door. "Ryan, I demand you put me down right this instant," she finally said, finally seeming to find her voice.

"Nicole, if you walk out that door now, you can kiss your job goodbye," her boss said. Ryan smiled as he walked out the door with her in his arms. She wasn't walking out the door, he was carrying her.

The few customers in the restaurant heard Ryan talking to Bubba, so no one was stepping up to stop him. He felt Nicole shudder as he carried her out the door and approached his car. From inside, Ryan could hear Nicole's boss yelling at her that she was fired.

Nicole pounded on Ryan's back in anger as they stepped up to his car. His driver opened the back door like there was nothing wrong with him carrying a girl over his shoulder. Hell, for all she knew, he did it on a regular basis. He tossed her down on the back seat and quickly climbed in beside her before she had the chance to get her breath back again.

CHAPTER TWO

Ryan said something to the driver, and the car started to move through the nearly deserted streets. Nicole was in shock from his behavior. She couldn't believe she'd been openly kidnapped in the middle of a diner and no one had done a thing to stop it.

"What do you think you're doing?" she demanded once she got her wind back.

"You wanted to talk, and then you walked out. You're lucky I'm giving you a second chance," he stated in an arrogant tone of voice. She looked at him like he was insane. He thought he was doing her a favor by dragging her out of the diner, costing her a valuable job and most likely her last paycheck as well.

"Are you insane? Do you know how difficult it is to find work?" she demanded.

"That was a crap job, and you know it. I did you a favor," he said. His tone of voice said he really did think he'd done her a favor. She rolled her eyes at him and sat back in the car, crossing her arms across her chest and glaring out the window. She had no idea where he was taking her, or even what to say to him.

Ryan watched her, as she did her best to pretend like he wasn't even there. He was irritated by her, acting as if he'd committed some crime when what he'd done was help her out. She was much better off without an unsafe job, and she'd soon be thanking him. He grinned as he thought about how she could thank him properly.

He was irritated by how much he desired her. He'd wanted her more than life itself when they'd been teenagers, but they'd both been far too young and had never cemented their relationship. They'd certainly done some heavy petting, but he'd never taken her and made her his. He was ready to rectify that.

The car pulled up to his gate and slipped inside for the long ride up his private driveway. Nicole seemed to tense more, as she realized they weren't on the main road anymore.

"Where are you taking me, Ryan?"

"To my house, so we can finish our chat privately," he simply replied.

Nicole looked at him nervously. She'd been in no way prepared to step into his house. It was truly his domain, and she didn't want to leave the vehicle. The driver pulled up to the massive home and opened the back door. She stubbornly sat there, refusing to exit the vehicle.

"You can get out and walk in, or I can carry you," Ryan said. The driver said nothing, and Nicole knew Ryan wasn't bluffing, so she reluctantly exited the car and followed him toward the house.

He opened the front door, and she stood there in shock. If she hadn't already known Ryan was incredibly wealthy, the sheer size of his home would've clued her in. She didn't understand why he'd need a place so large. The entryway alone was bigger than the house she'd grown up in. She looked around in awe and desperately tried to tamp down her reaction. She could feel Ryan's eyes on her, and she didn't want to give him the satisfaction of knowing she was impressed by his wealth.

Nicole was suddenly so exhausted she could barely even stand, let alone walk the long hallway they were traversing. The house seemed to be endless, but she placed one foot in front of the other as she followed him deeper into the home.

Finally they rounded a turn, and he led her into an inviting room with a warm fire crackling.

She didn't ask him permission. She simply walked over to the comfortable looking sofa and got off her aching feet. Soon, a woman walked into the room and placed a tray near her, which had a steaming cup of coffee on it along with cream and sugar. She doctored up a cup and took a revitalizing sip. It was pure heaven. She hadn't had such good coffee in forever.

Before she realized it, the entire cup was gone, and Ryan was taking it away and placing a new cup in front of her. She prepared the coffee the way she liked it and sat back, sipping more slowly on her second cup. She didn't know what was in it, but her eyes were feeling even heavier than before, and her body was in a complete state of relaxation.

"Are you feeling better?" Ryan asked, snapping her out of her trance.

"This must be decaffeinated because I'm having a hard time staying awake," she answered him.

"It has a shot of rum in it to soothe your nerves," he answered with a slight nod. Nicole was irritated with him for doing that without her permission, but the liquor was doing its job, and she felt too relaxed to yell at him. "I need to make a call, so we'll talk when I get back," he said and left her alone in the room. Nicole breathed out a sigh of relief. She wanted nothing more than to simply relax for a few minutes before they had the conversation.

She knew she needed to ask for his help with her sister and she was more confident he'd help, but she wasn't sure if she was going to be able to handle whatever he wanted out of her in return. She was beginning to think he was going to want his pound of flesh. She shuddered as she sat back and closed her eyes. Her mind drifted back to that awful day so many years before.

She'd been sixteen years old, and he was eighteen. They'd dated for about a year, and she was head over heels in love with him. That had been the summer things had gone to hell with her family. Her father had always been abusive, but he'd worked full-time and she'd managed to keep

Ryan away from him. Her mother had been around, but she wasn't much of a parent.

When her father lost his job, the abuse had gone to a whole new level, and she realized she couldn't possibly keep a boyfriend without him realizing what was going on. Her father was taking out his aggravation on her daily, and her body showed obvious signs. Her mother had decided to step out of reality by drowning herself in alcohol from morning to night. Nicole was miserable and in no way wanted the boy she was in love with to realize what a pathetic person she'd become.

She'd planned on running away with Ryan when he headed to the city. She'd work while he went to college and they could marry and have a nice little house with a white picket fence. Those dreams were lost because she couldn't leave her baby sister behind. If she wasn't there to protect Patsy, her sister would be the one taking the beatings instead of her, and that wasn't acceptable. Patsy was only four at the time.

When she realized she had to break up with him she wanted him to think it was because she was a selfish teenager instead of a pathetic one. She led him to believe she didn't think he was good enough for her. She played her role well, and he walked away without once looking back. He'd always been self-conscious of his poor roots and, to the outside world, her family seemed well off.

By the time Ryan left, things had gotten really bad at home. He was out of school, and though she'd seen him a few times in town, he acted like she didn't even exist. It nearly destroyed her when she ran into him with another girl hanging on his arm. He'd spotted her and sent her a wink and she walked away, trying to seem casual. Then she threw up once she was out of sight of him.

Ryan had left two years after they broke up, seemingly hating her as much as the day she'd broken up with him. She'd endured the abuse for another two years after his departure. Once she turned eighteen, she got a decent job, took her sister and moved out. Her father didn't try to stop her because he was afraid of going to jail, and her mother was too gone to even notice her daughters had left.

Her parents died in an automobile crash two years later, and it had only been her and Patsy from that point on. They'd been scraping by-- doing fine until Patsy got heart disease which threatened to take her life. Nicole fell asleep with her old memories fresh in her mind, exhaustion finally taking her away. She didn't want to think about the hurtful past or about her present condition.

###

Ryan walked into the den and found Nicole asleep on the couch. She looked so exhausted, with the dark circles under her eyes and her body lying limp against the back of the couch. His anger was deflated at the sight of her.

He scooped her into his arms, and in her sleep she turned to him, seeking his protection. She wrapped herself around him, causing his body to stir with desire. He was disgusted with himself for being so affected, with little more than a simple movement from Nicole in her sleep.

He placed her on his huge bed, and she began to shiver. He quickly pulled off her shoes and pants, groaning at the small scrap of her panties visible to him. He quickly covered her up and decided there was no way he could walk away.

He took a very cold shower and, still not trusting himself, put on a pair of sweats and climbed in next to her. She immediately curled into him, and he held her for hours while his body ached. Eventually, he relaxed and drifted into a dreamless sleep.

Nicole woke up and stretched her arms. She felt more rested, which was a wonderful feeling. She slowly opened her eyes and realized she was in a very comfortable--and yet unfamiliar--bed. She looked around in a bit of a panic, not knowing where she was. She was used to waking up in unfamiliar places — since she'd been a nomad for months--but she'd never awakened somewhere so luxurious.

"I didn't think you would ever wake up," Ryan's voice said. She jerked up in bed and suddenly remembered her strange night with him. She didn't have a clue how she'd ended up in one of his beds but was eternally grateful to discover she wasn't naked. She then noticed her missing pants and felt the blush rush over her cheeks. Had he been the one to take her pants off? She was wearing perfectly fine panties that wouldn't have shown him much, but she was still a bit mortified.

"How did I get here?" she managed to choke out.

"I carried you," he answered and had the gall to wink at her. She couldn't stop her face from flaming even redder. "I'll give you some privacy to shower and get dressed. Meet me downstairs in the den," he told her and disappeared out the door. She'd never been so grateful for someone to leave.

She slowly climbed from the bed and took her time in his shower. If he insisted on her being in his place and treating her like a child, then he could wait on her, she thought, a bit too smugly. With no other reason to delay, she slowly made her way down the huge staircase in search of the den. She didn't have to look too long because her nose led the way. She smelled something that made her stomach growl and reminded her she hadn't eaten since breakfast twenty-four hours earlier.

She stepped into the den, and her eyes were drawn to a side table with several dishes on it, filled with delicious smelling food. She wanted so badly to step over to the table and grab a plate full of food, but she wasn't even a guest in the house and couldn't bring herself to do it.

Ryan watched her look longingly at the food. She heard him blow out a breath of frustration.

"Would you please quit staring at the food as if it will disappear and get yourself a plate? We can talk over breakfast," he said. She jumped when she heard his voice.

"Thank you," she muttered. She didn't have to be told twice. Nicole dug into the food like it was her last meal. Heck, the way she lived, it could be a while before she was able to eat this well again, and she knew it. She didn't even care if she looked like a complete pig. She was going to eat until her stomach hurt. She really didn't care what he'd have to say about it.

Nicole sat at the table and began eating as if it were a race. Unfortunately, her stomach had shrunk over the months, and she wasn't even able to finish a quarter of the food she'd placed on her plate. His housekeeper came and tried to clear her plate, and Nicole almost growled at her. The woman looked up, startled.

"I'm not done yet," she said. She could feel the awful red flushing her cheeks again.

"Let Maria take the plate, and if you get hungry again, then you can grab some fresh food," Ryan said with a little chuckle. Nicole glared at him, snagged the muffin off the plate and reluctantly let his housekeeper take the rest away.

"Okay, I think it's time to have our chat now," Ryan told her. Nicole took a deep breath and got ready to beg. There was no one, other than her sister, who she'd lower herself for. Since she was more of a mother to Patsy than a sibling, she'd do whatever it took to make sure she'd be okay.

"Patsy has a rare heart disease requiring surgery, but her insurance doesn't cover it. They say it's an elective surgery and yet, if she doesn't get it, she won't survive to her seventeenth birthday," Nicole said in a rush. She was fighting tears at even speaking of the thought of losing Patsy. She loved her so much and she was supposed to take care of her. She was supposed to be the one who made sure Patsy didn't get sick, and now Patsy was barely hanging on. The thought of it nearly destroyed Nicole.

"So you need to borrow money?" He leaned back in his chair and was looking at Nicole like she was a piece of meat he was about to devour. She had to fight not to glare at him.

"It's killing me to borrow money from you. I just need someone to pay her surgery costs. I'll get a new job right away and pay every dime of it back," she said stubbornly. She couldn't tell from his expression if he was going to do it or not. The waiting was killing her.

"What are you willing to do for me if I do this?" he asked coldly.

"I . . . I don't understand," she stuttered.

"Come on, Nicole. You're so much smarter than this, or at least you used to be. Money means nothing to me. I can pay the bill without it even placing a dent in my wallet, so I don't need — nor want — you to pay me back," he told her in a smug tone of voice.

"What do you want?" she asked, afraid of the answer he might give. He smiled, and her stomach clenched. She was terrified of what was going to come out of his mouth next. What if the thing he wanted wasn't possible for her to give? If it was within her power, then of course she'd do it, but she couldn't figure out what he could possibly want from her. She had absolutely nothing.

Ryan knew he was going straight to hell, but he didn't care. He wanted her, and now he had the chance to get what he wanted. He'd get from her what he wanted and, when he was finished, he'd walk away. Then maybe he wouldn't feel the ache.

She'd never know he'd already arranged the surgery and moved Patsy the night before.

She didn't know that, even if she walked right out the door and told him to go to hell, he'd still help Patsy. He'd loved that little girl. He'd help her without requiring anything. On the other hand, why not get something out of Nicole if he could? He looked straight into her eyes so there would be no chance of a misunderstanding.

"I want you in my house — in my bed — at my beck and call. You'll be here for me night and day, for whatever I need until I'm bored with you. Then I'll set both you and Patsy up in a decent place since apparently you're homeless at the moment and have nowhere for her to recover," he told her. He added the last part to drive home her desperate need of his help.

He watched her expression as his words registered. Her eyes widened in comprehension and, if he would've seen only horror in her expression, he would've backed off, but it wasn't the only thing he saw. He saw passion in her eyes and a quickening of her breath at his words. She wanted him. He was sure of it. He'd bet his entire fortune on it. He also knew the moment he won. He saw the slump of her shoulders, and she lowered her eyes in defeat.

"I require an answer — now," he commanded. He didn't want to give her any time to change her mind.

"What choice are you giving me?" she yelled as a tear slipped down her cheek.

Ryan refused to be swayed by her tears. For all he knew, she was letting the water works fall, as all women did, to get her own way. He turned from her and poured himself a shot of bourbon. He knew it was much too early in the day for a drink, but it was either that or pull her into his arms, and he wanted to save that for later.

"You'll, of course, move in immediately as you have nowhere else to go, and you'll act as if you're completely over the moon for me when we're out in public. I think we'll get along fine as long as you do as I say," he told her with an expression that said he was completely serious.

He saw a shudder run through Nicole's body, and he wondered what had caused it. Was she that afraid of being with him? He'd seen such desire in her eyes only moments before.

"I need to see my sister," was all she said.

"We can head over there now. Her surgery has already been arranged," he told her.

Nicole's head snapped up, and she glared at him.. "You were so sure of yourself?" she finally said.

Ryan smiled at the words. She was finding some of her backbone once again. "I didn't have any doubt you'd put your sister ahead of yourself. After all, you've always been willing to self-sacrifice," he mocked her.

Nicole stood up, turned on her heels and started to leave. Before she'd made it more than a few steps, he was there, whipping her around to face him. They glared at one another, neither willing to back down.

###

"I think the occasion needs to be sealed with a kiss," Ryan practically purred at her. Before Nicole had any time to react to his statement, his lips pressed down onto hers, and her world exploded.

She refused to open up to him at first but, as his tongue flicked along the seam of her lips, she quickly lost her willpower. He pressed her lower back into his body, where she could feel his obvious arousal, causing a gasp to escape her lips, giving him access to her mouth. He dipped his tongue inside, and all thoughts of resisting him dissipated.

His hands ran up and down her quivering body, and he had her melting in a matter of seconds. No other man had ever kissed her like Ryan, and she was grateful he was holding her up because her legs would've given way long ago. Before she knew what she was doing, her arms wrapped around his neck to pull him closer, and she fell into the kiss with a passion that shocked both of them.

He continued to love her mouth with his tongue, while his hands worked their own magic on her needy body. She wanted more and wiggled as close as she could possibly get to him. She cursed the clothes that kept them separated.

He finally pulled away from her, and she whimpered her displeasure of him doing so. His glazed eyes came back into focus as he looked down at her flushed cheeks and beaded nipples, which had been pressed so tightly against him moments before. She started to regain her composure, realizing how wanton she'd acted, and he saw the shutters fly over her eyes. He lifted a brow at her, which caused her temper to boil.

"I think this arrangement will work out just fine, as long as you continue to be such a tempting little thing," he said with mockery in his tone.

"You really are despicable," she lashed back at him. He laughed at her temper, and she saw in his eyes that he was turned on by it. Her glare hardened. Ryan released her suddenly, and Nicole almost crumbled to the floor. Only her sheer willpower kept her standing straight.

"I may be despicable, but you want me, and this will be mutually pleasurable," he drawled.

"Or I'm just one fine actress," she said, while smiling sweetly. She then made a very hasty exit when she saw the murderous expression enter his eyes. She locked herself into a bathroom, where she stayed until she had her breathing under control and her features blanked. She wouldn't let him know how much he affected her. He already had too much power. She couldn't give him her control too.

Ryan thought about chasing her down and proving to her there was no way in hell she'd been acting. He'd felt her coming apart in his arms from a simple kiss. When he finally took her to his bed and made her his, she'd be screaming out his name.

He would've done just that if he was more in control of himself. As it was, he could barely stand and was afraid the day ahead would be a painful one. She did things to his body no other woman had ever been able to. He wanted her, and that night he'd finally have her. He'd never wanted a day to end so badly.

When she finally returned to the den, they both looked at one another coolly. He'd let her have some space, only because he needed it as well. She gathered her purse, and they left for the hospital. He had all day to anticipate the night to come.

CHAPTER THREE

"I missed you last night, Nik," Patsy said when the two of them stepped into the room.

"I'm so sorry, Hun. I got caught up at work, but I came as early as I could this morning," Nicole said to her sister. "You probably don't remember Ryan," she added.

"Ryan, is that you?" Patsy asked, and a huge smile spread across her hollow features. Ryan couldn't believe how weak and small she looked. She'd been full of life as a young toddler and, though she was beautiful, she looked so ill it nearly brought him to his knees. He sat on the edge of the bed, and she eagerly took his hand.

"I'm sorry you've been in so much pain," Ryan told her with a suspicious tightness in his throat. He tried to clear it, uncomfortable with the feeling.

"I missed you," she told him, almost accusatory.

"I've missed you too, little one, and I'm sorry I haven't been there for you," Ryan told her.

"I'm glad you're here now," she said with a child's honesty.

"Me too," he said, surprised by how much he meant the words.

"Are you and Nicole together again?" she asked hopefully.

"We are," he simply stated.

"That's so cool. Nicole has always loved you," she said with the innocence of youth. Ryan looked over at Nicole, who was blushing scarlet.

She glared at him and shook her head before turning to her sister."You're going to get your operation, baby," Nicole told her. Ryan saw the tears well up in her eyes.

"Really?" Patsy asked with disbelief as she looked from Ryan to Nicole.

"Really," Ryan told her. She held out her arms, and he gently pulled her close. She was even tinier than he'd originally thought. His heart ached as he felt her tiny frame through the thin hospital gown.

Ryan and Nicole sat in Patsy's room for hours, visiting and keeping her spirits up, until she could no longer stay awake. She fought going to sleep, but she finally drifted off. Ryan quietly led Nicole from the room.

###

No words were spoken as they walked from the hospital. He led her to his car, and they made their way back to his home. She'd been able to dampen down the nerves while she was visiting with her sister, but now she was nervous. She knew he expected her to sleep with him, and she didn't know how to respond to his request.

They pulled up to the house and there were a couple of cars in the driveway. Ryan blew out a breath of frustration when he spotted the vehicles, giving Nicole a look she didn't understand.

"Well, now we are going to test your acting skills. Remember what you agreed to," he snapped at her before leading her from the vehicle. She looked at him quizzically and followed him into the house.

"About time you got back, Ryan. Did you forget about the barbecue?" Derek said as he stepped around the corner.

Nicole got a shock as she saw Derek and Drew, a couple of women, and some kids. She stood there like a doe in headlights, not knowing what to say. She hadn't seen Ryan's cousins since they were all kids. She'd once loved them so much and, although they'd tried speaking to her after she and Ryan broke up, she'd found it too painful and cut all ties.

"Is that you, Nicole? I haven't seen you in forever. You look great," Drew said when he realized who was standing next to his cousin. Before she knew what was happening, Drew walked over and engulfed her in a huge bear hug. She felt the tears stinging her eyes at the easy acceptance he offered.

"Now who's this gorgeous woman you're mauling?" Trinity asked good-naturedly.

"Trinity, this is Nicole. She and Ryan used to be all hot and heavy when we were teenagers. Nicole, this beautiful woman is my wife, Trinity," Drew introduced them.

"It's so nice to meet you, Nicole," Trinity said and shocked Nicole by stepping forward and giving her a big hug.

"It's nice to meet you, too," Nicole said shyly.

"Now it's my turn, stranger," Derek said and stepped forward, lifting her off her feet and spinning her around. "It's so great to see you."

Jasmine stepped around the corner and spotted Nicole. "I haven't seen you in forever," she said, throwing her arms around her. Nicole hugged her back, grateful to see a familiar female face. "How have you been?"

"I'm great," Nicole told her. "I didn't know you and Derek got back together," she added. She remembered the devastation Jasmine had felt when Derek left her so many years ago. Nicole had been feeling her own pain from one of the Titan cousins and had sympathized completely.

"Yes, and it's been amazing. It looks like these Titan boys are finally waking up," Jasmine told her with a wink. Nicole didn't know what to say.

"Yes, Nicole and I ran into each other again, and we realized we simply couldn't live one more second apart," Ryan said. Nicole thought only she could hear the sarcasm in his tone. She had to fight not to flinch when he gave her a look that seemed to threaten her not to contradict him. She turned away from him, finding it difficult to look into his eyes.

"Well, we have to catch up and figure out ways to torture these men," Jasmine said and led the other two women away, leaving the men to watch them go.

###

"So what's going on with you? I adore Nicole. You know that, but I still remember the utter devastation you felt when she walked out of your life," Drew asked his cousin. Ryan wasn't ready to tell his cousins the truth. It made him too much of a cad, and he didn't want to see the disapproving look in their eyes.

"We ran into each other and realized the spark was still there, so we decided to pursue it," he finally said. He thought they may take exception to the fact that, in reality, he was blackmailing her into his bed. Hell, he'd kick their asses if they did the same thing. It was much easier to notice other people's flaws than your own, and he wanted her too badly to stop what he was doing, even knowing how wrong it was.

"She's even more gorgeous now than she was as a teenager," Derek said with a wiggle of his brows.

"Back off. You're a married man," Ryan told his cousin, feeling an irrational urge to mark his claim. He knew Derek was a happily married man, but Ryan found he didn't like any man making a comment about Nicole. Derek simply laughed at his cousin before the three of them headed off toward the pool.

###

"So spill, Nicole. We want all the juicy details of how you two got together and what you've been up to," Jasmine demanded of Nicole.

Nicole actually felt herself relaxing, sitting in the presence of a familiar face and a new friend. There was something very reassuring about having women to talk with who were nice and understanding.

She found she wanted to spill her guts to them but was afraid Ryan would be furious and then would refuse to help her sister. She didn't think he'd stop the surgery, but she wasn't taking any chances. She still had feelings for Ryan, so she could be as honest as possible.

"My sister's in the hospital, and I didn't have anyone to turn to or talk with, so I called Ryan. He was there instantly, and the minute I saw him again all those old feelings came right back to the surface," Nicole said in as simple an explanation as she could.

"Your sister's in the hospital? What's wrong with her? How can we help?" Jasmine fired off a bunch of questions with a look of concern on her face. Nicole explained about the heart surgery and, before long, she was crying with Jasmine and Trinity. It was so nice to have someone to lean on and to listen to her cry out her heartache. Nicole had been holding it all in for the last several months.

She hadn't allowed herself to break down and cry even once because she knew, if she were to let go, she wouldn't be able to pick herself back up again. She realized she wasn't falling completely apart, though. She was actually feeling supported by the two amazing women.

The men walked in, saw the three teary women, and were instantly on alert. They looked at one another in a panic and knelt down.

"What's wrong, Baby?" Derek asked with concern.

"You don't need to worry, Derek. We're simply women, and this is what we do," Jasmine told her husband with a watery smile.

"You know we have to try and fix it," Drew added as he rubbed along Trinity's back.

"That's because you're the most honorable men we know, but we really will be okay," Trinity said.

"Now, boys, give us more time together, and then we'll start making dinner," Jasmine said to the men. They reluctantly walked away, though they mumbled to each other about emotional women.

Jasmine and Trinity continued to comfort Nicole until all the tears ran dry. They slowly pulled themselves together and headed toward the kitchen. There was a household staff who normally cooked, but sometimes it was soothing to prepare a meal together.

"I hear Joshua crying. I'll be right back," Trinity said, walking over to grab her infant from his car seat.

"He's beautiful," Nicole said with longing. She'd never allowed herself to even think about having a baby. You had to have a relationship first, and she didn't have the time for one.

"He's only three months old. Jasmine and I had our youngest within a few weeks of each other, and it's been great to share the experience," Trinity told her as she brought her son close to nurse.

Jasmine pulled her son Jaxon out of his car seat. He was awake but not hungry yet. Nicole wanted to hold him with an ache that surprised her, but she didn't want to be forward and ask. As if Jasmine could read her mind, she handed over her son, and Nicole sighed in pleasure.

"Oh, I haven't held such a tiny baby since Patsy was a newborn," Nicole said in awe as she rubbed his precious cheek. "He's so little," she added in complete awe.

"They're a lot of work but worth every single minute, and Derek is such an attentive and amazing father. He shares the nights with me, making everything perfect. There are many people who are disgusted with us," Jasmine gushed.

"I don't know of many men who are up for the three a.m. feedings," Trinity added. "Drew is just as amazing at helping me out. I couldn't imagine doing this all on my own."

"Do you get to stay at home with them?" Nicole asked.

"We own a shop together but only spend minimal time there, and the babies always come with us. Ryan built us an amazing nursery and a play structure for the older kids. We get to have a business that's ours. We take pride in it but still get to be the kind of mothers we want to be," Trinity told her. Nicole was filled with a bit of envy, which she instantly felt guilty about.

It would be so heavenly to not have any worries and get to be a full-time mother. She felt more like a mom to Patsy instead of a big sister, and she wished she'd been able to be with her more, but she always worked hard to keep a roof over their heads and to have the supplies Patsy needed to get a good education. She'd spent every free moment with her, though, which was another reason she didn't date. She really had a full plate.

The sad thing was, she didn't think she'd ever get to hold her own child in her arms. *Maybe someday*, she thought wistfully. The women continued to visit, and Nicole got her baby fix, holding little Jaxon in her arms.

The men slowly walked into the kitchen like it was a war zone. They were afraid the women were going to send them away again, and the alpha males didn't like the feeling of being told to go away. They crept through the doorway, and there was an audible sigh of relief from all three men when they saw the women laughing. They once again looked at each other as if they really couldn't understand the complicated minds of women. The women saw the faces of the men and exchanged knowing glances. The men would never know why one minute, they were sobbing together, and the next minute, they were laughing as if all was right with the world. That was just one difference between the sexes that would always exist.

"Can we help you with anything?" Derek questioned.

"You can get the steak going. The rest of this food will be ready before you know it," Trinity told them. They grabbed the marinated steaks and made a quick exit. The girls giggled at the guy's haste.

"I know it's terrible to play with them, but sometimes it's simply way too much fun not to," Jasmine said with a giggle.

"Agreed," Trinity said. Nicole nodded, although she was afraid to play with Ryan. She had a feeling, if she tried to play, she was going to get seriously burned. She put it out of her mind and simply enjoyed her time of peace in a world which had been shattered for many years.

They all enjoyed a wonderful meal, then sat by a fire, where Nicole found herself laughing more than she'd ever done in her life. The cousins were certainly entertaining and Nicole forgot, for a small moment in time, how much stress she was under. When it was past midnight, the family headed out, and she was uncomfortably aware she was alone with Ryan. She didn't know how to behave, or what to say.

"I'm really tired, so if you could tell me where I'm sleeping, I'll leave you alone," she mumbled at him.

"You'll be sleeping in my bed again, but this time I won't lie awake half the night in frustration," he growled at her.

"I'm not sleeping in your bed, Ryan," she said with her own rising temper. He couldn't force her to sleep with him.

Ryan glared at her and slowly stood up. He seemed more of a predator than she'd ever seen before. She was somewhat terrified but more aroused than she'd ever admit. He was an impressively masculine man and, with that look of desire mixed with fury in his eyes, her stomach turned into a quivering mass.

Ryan slowly started stalking toward her, and she couldn't help herself from slowly retreating. She wanted to stand firm, but she was too afraid of what would happen if he touched her. She wasn't convinced of her own willpower.

"Ryan, you need to back off. I know we have an agreement, but I'm tired and not ready to share your bed yet," Nicole tried to reason with him, still backing away as he made a steady advance toward her. He said nothing as he continued to stalk her, as if she really was his prey. He didn't speed up. He didn't yell. He did nothing but follow her.

She looked behind her and realized he was backing her into a corner. She knew it was the chicken's way out, but she didn't care. If she didn't flee the room really soon, he was going to grab her, and she knew if that happened, she'd be lost.

She noticed the table to her left, made a dash around it, and started running from the room. She could call herself a chicken later. Her only thought was getting into another room--one with a lock where she wouldn't be tempted to let him take her to bed.

She'd just made it to the bottom of the stairs when his fingers locked around her wrist. He whipped her around, jerking her body against his and smiling in triumph, only seconds before his mouth fell on hers. She was panting from her short sprint, leaving her mouth open to his probing tongue. She gasped aloud as his tongue stroked her mouth, causing liquid fire to burn through her veins.

She'd kissed him countless times as a teenager, but it had in no way prepared her for the kiss of a man. He was devastating her system in a matter of seconds. She tried to pull out of his arms. She tried to regain her composure, but he was touching her in a way that rushed all thoughts from her mind. Suddenly he picked her up in his arms, while continuing to love her mouth. She was losing all will of saying no to the man.

He carried her quickly up the stairs and, before Nicole knew what was happening, he was laying her down on the bed, and her clothes were stripped away. Ryan lay alongside her, quickly taking her back in his arms and once again locking his lips down on hers.

She needed to stop him. She needed to let him know she wasn't ready. She needed to gain the willpower to stop, but she couldn't do it. She couldn't even think, let alone find the strength to deny him and herself.

Ryan released her mouth, only to trail his lips down her neck and run his tongue along the mounds of her breasts. By the time he finally clasped her aching nipple into his mouth, her entire body jerked off the bed. She was done with any protests she'd thought about issuing. He ran his tongue over her nipples, and she could feel the tightening in her stomach and the wetness in her core. Her body was preparing for his entrance, and she wanted him more than she wanted anything else.

He was making her feel completely possessed with his domination of her body. She was weak to his every command. He continued circling her chest with his tongue, and she could do nothing but moan in pleasure as her hands rubbed over his body. She could feel the slight sheen of sweat on his skin, which only turned her on more, to witness his loss of ever-present control. She'd brought him to a state of arousal with nothing more than her responses to him.

She could feel his impressive erection pressing into her thigh, and her body squirmed underneath him, needing to feel him press against her core. She needed him to join them together, and she couldn't wait much longer.

"I've wanted to do this since the first kiss we shared," he confided in a ragged voice. His tone made her squirm even more. Nicole could feel that he was on the edge of control, and she didn't mind being the one to push him over the cliff.

He brought his lips back to hers and kissed her so tenderly, she was washed away with emotions. How could he be so cold and calculating one moment and kiss her as if she was the most precious thing in the universe the next? If she hadn't already been past the point of no return, that kiss would've done it.

He pressed the head of his erection against her slick opening, and she could feel the heat burning in her aching core. "Please," she begged him, when he still wouldn't thrust inside her.

###

"I can't wait any longer," he growled at her. He wanted to make it good for her. He wanted to make sure she was ready for him, but he'd wanted her for so long and hadn't been with any other in months, and there was no way he could drag out their lovemaking.

He lifted her leg, pushing it behind his back, opening her up fully for him. He could feel her heat against his head, and it was making his entire body break out in a sweat. He struggled to maintain his control. He'd never before lost control of his body with any other woman.

He heard Nicole gasp as the intense pleasure washed through her. She jerked her hips, and Ryan knew she was trying to get him to enter her.

He didn't need any more prompting. With one quick thrust, he buried himself fully in her. She tensed as his entire girth filled her fully.

Ryan groaned at the tightness of her body gripping him. He couldn't believe how hard she was holding onto him. It sent him all the way over the edge of sanity and, after a small pause, he pulled out of her and thrust back in, working faster with each move. He was out of control as he gripped her hips, raising her higher so he could sink even further inside.

###

After the initial shock and slight pain of him filling her up, Nicole felt nothing but pleasure. She soon lifted her hips up to meet his thrusts. She could feel her body tightening more and more with each thrust inside of her.

Suddenly, a pleasure unlike anything she'd ever felt before was gripping her body. Nicole cried out as the lightning shot through her core, up through her stomach and down each limb. She was shaking from head to toe as the orgasm kept rippling through her in spasm after spasm.

Within seconds, Ryan was buried deeper inside her, shooting his pleasure deep within her core. He pumped into her for longer than he'd ever done before, then he collapsed against her body, as if he didn't have the energy to move a limb. Nicole knew she'd completely drained him.

A few minutes later, Ryan must've realized he was crushing her, and he managed to turn them both on their sides with their bodies still connected. They slid along one another since they both had a sheen of sweat all over their bodies. They were both panting as if they'd run a marathon. Nicole couldn't believe what an amazing experience that had been, and she was almost regretful she'd waited so long. She had a feeling, though, that it wouldn't have been the same with any other man except Ryan. She'd never felt such intense emotions for any other man but him, which was most likely how she'd managed to remain a virgin well into her twenties.

Ryan finally pulled out of her body, and she felt as if she lost a piece of herself. She grumbled at him, which caused a chuckle to escape his throat. She tensed at his laughter, but she was so tired, she couldn't manage to pull away or even open her eyes to glare at him.

She'd allow herself to lie there for a few more moments before she got up and found another bed. She refused to give him her heart or soul, even if he had her body. If she slept with him nightly, she was afraid he'd get both. She fell asleep with those frightening thoughts on her mind.

Ryan woke up and found himself alone in the bed, and he wasn't happy about it. He'd left the bed of many clingy women but found he didn't like being the one left. He threw the covers off him, getting ready to track Nicole down and bring her back. He got up and twisted around, and then his heartbeat stopped.

He looked closer at the bed and saw the blood. Had he hurt her without knowing? The thought was incomprehensible. He thought about their lovemaking. He'd taken her a bit roughly and noticed her tensing but assumed it may have been a while for her, so he'd given her a few moments to adjust to him. He knew she was unbelievably tight, but she couldn't possibly have been a virgin. There was no way a woman could reach her age without losing her innocence, but the evidence was staring him straight in the face.

His legs wouldn't support him, so he sank down on the bed in shock. He'd thought she'd dumped him as a teenager to explore her options and date guys she thought were better than him, and he'd been filled with rage. As he thought back, he realized he hadn't seen her with one other guy after him. He'd been so angry with her he'd never thought much about it.

There had to be another explanation for the blood because there was no way she'd been innocent. He threw it from his mind because the other option made him far too much of a jerk. He couldn't face that. She'd been the one to dump him without ever looking back, and she deserved to suffer a bit. It wasn't like she wasn't getting to live in the lap of luxury on her own, so she was getting something out of the arrangement as well. He went to hunt her down, so she'd be perfectly aware of where she belonged.

CHAPTER FOUR

Nicole was abruptly awakened by a very angry-looking Ryan. She'd woken up after the second time he'd taken her in the middle of the night and had waited for him to fall asleep before she'd snuck from his bed to find another room. It hadn't been hard, as the place seemed to have an endless supply of spare rooms.

"What do you think you're doing in here?" he demanded after staring at her in silence for several minutes.

"I was trying to sleep," she snapped back and turned over and lay back down, shutting her eyes.

Ryan ripped the blanket off her body, which caused her to sit straight up in bed, no longer pretending to be sleepy. She glared at him.

"You'll be sleeping all night in my bed," he told her.

"I'll sleep where I want to," she stated.

"You're the most insufferable woman I've ever met in my life. Did you forget we have an agreement? Did you think I'd simply fork out a ton of my own money, set you up in my home and get nothing in return?" he demanded. She flinched at his words and the rage behind them.

"You got what you wanted last night," she finally spat, still humiliated she'd so easily caved to him. A shiver ran down her spine as she thought about the way she'd responded.

"I'll continue to get what I want, and what I want is you in my bed every night--all night," he told her as he leaned down on the bed in front of her. She glared back at him, with her arms crossed against her chest. "Do you understand?" he asked, only inches from her face.

"Yes," she spat, willing to say about anything to get him to back off and give her some breathing space. He smiled triumphantly and closed the space between them. She gasped in shock at the passion of the kiss and, before she'd had time to react, he pulled away and walked from the room.

Nicole sat there, trembling on the bed. She wasn't sure if she was relieved he'd left or not. She couldn't deny she wanted him, but that was natural, as she'd been head over heels in love with him at one of the darkest times in her life. She'd depended on him and needed him, and she'd ended up having to let him go, for fear of him pitying her. There would've been nothing worse.

She slowly got up and headed back to his room to find her clothing. It was mercifully in the closet. She looked at her few pathetic items and hung her head down. She'd been living with only a few outfits for as long as she could remember. Her sister's needs had been so much more important than her own. Patsy had never been aware of the sacrifices she'd made because there was no reason for her to know. Nicole was only doing what any sister should do in her circumstances.

Nicole made her way downstairs and headed straight for the food. She was once again starving and filled her plate. She ate a bit more than she had the day before, but her stomach was still not used to having a full meal. There was a secure feeling in knowing she'd have a warm meal in the morning. She'd rather have that guarantee than a full dinner.

"We need to get going so we can see Patsy before she's taken into surgery," Ryan told her. She stuffed the toast in her mouth and jumped up.

"I'm ready," she told him through her mouthful of food and walked toward the front door. Ryan followed her, and they had a silent drive to the hospital. Nicole had to tell herself she was doing the right thing and nothing else mattered except for her sister getting better. It was hard to remember anything when she was in the small space with Ryan, though.

His scent invaded her senses and caused her stomach to tighten with need. Even when she was mad at him, she still wanted to be near him, and she still wanted to feel his touch. She tried to convince herself she was simply exhausted and, when her sister was better, she wouldn't feel the pull toward him. She'd worried about everything for so long she needed some worry-free days. Her body needed time to recharge itself.

Patsy was alert and nervous when they stepped into her room. It took a while for them to calm her down, especially considering Nicole was just as nervous as Patsy was. When they wheeled her into the surgery room, Nicole couldn't say a word. She was close to bursting into tears.

"The surgery's going to take a couple of hours, so why don't we go out to lunch? You need to get your mind off of what's going on," Ryan suggested as they walked toward the waiting area.

"No, I need to be here in case the doctor comes out," she said in almost a panic.

"We can stay. That's fine," Ryan offered. They stepped through the doors, and Nicole was amazed to find his whole family sitting in there — all of them, including his cousins, their spouses and both of his uncles. The women jumped up and immediately threw their arms around her, causing the tears she refused to let fall to come cascading down her cheeks. Nicole was scared, and so she was very happy to let Jasmine and Trinity comfort her.

"What are you doing here?" she finally managed to ask. After all, Patsy wasn't related to them. She was more than grateful for their presence, though.

"We couldn't let you go through this on your own," Jasmine said, as if she was crazy to think anything differently. Nicole was more than willing to accept their love and support and continued to cry all her fears out into their arms.

Ryan found himself to be a third wheel, and he didn't like the feeling. He should be the one who she was turning to. It should have been his shoulder she was crying into. He wanted to kick himself when he had those thoughts because he normally hated clingy, emotional women and ran the second they behaved in that manner.

The men pulled him out of the room and walked him to the café to get some much-needed coffee. None of them said anything. They just drank some coffee and let the girls have some needed time together. Not one of them could possibly understand the female mind and felt safer at a distance, so that they didn't accidentally say something that might land them in hot water.

When they'd let enough time pass, they finally made their way back to the room with coffee and donuts to share. The women managed to get Nicole to drink the coffee, but no amount of pleading would get her to eat. Ryan was relieved the tears had at least dried up. He didn't know how to handle them.

###

The hours waiting for the doctor to come back in were the longest of Nicole's life. She paced up and down the hallways, waiting for him to bring her any information. She needed to know her baby sister was going to be okay, and Nicole wouldn't feel better until the moment she heard that news. Ryan tried to get her to eat something, but there was no way she could keep any food down. The breakfast she'd eaten was sitting uneasily in her stomach, and she feared she was going to vomit all over the pristine floors.

"Ms. Lander," a doctor said as he stepped into the room. She whipped her head around and looked at him with both fear and hope. Nothing could've happened to Patsy. She wouldn't survive it.

"Yes?" she said, barely above a whisper. She was terrified, but she needed to know.

"Your sister is out of surgery, and it looks like everything will be fine. The next few hours are critical, but it looks like your sister is going to make a full recovery," he told her.

"Thank you," she sobbed and threw her arms around the doctor, clinging tightly. He patted her back and whispered reassurances. She was so relieved the nightmare seemed to finally be over.

She had to see for herself Patsy was alive and breathing.

She finally managed to pull herself together and was led into Patsy's recovery room.

Ryan sent the rest of the family home, as Patsy wouldn't be awake more than minutes at a time. There wasn't any point in them staying at the hospital. They reluctantly left, and exhaustion took over Nicole as she lay in the chair next to Patsy's bed. She fell asleep for the first time in a long while, with peace in her heart.

The night was long, with Patsy only waking for short periods of time. Every time the nurses came in to check on her, they assured both Nicole and Ryan, who also refused to leave, that she was healing fine and that it looked like she'd be okay. Nicole wouldn't completely believe them until she walked out of the hospital, but she was happy.

"You're coming out with us today. You've done nothing but sit here and worry about your sister, and she's fine. She has a million magazines, doctors and nurses at her beck and call and food being brought in. You, on the other hand, look like you haven't eaten in a month, have dark circles

95

under your eyes and are in desperate need of a manicure," Jasmine said to Nicole the next morning.

Nicole stared at the two women before her, feeling slightly shell-shocked. They were trying to get her to leave the hospital room, but she'd feel guilty doing so. Patsy needed her there, and Nicole had an irrational fear that, if she left her side, something would happen to her.

"I can't leave her," she pleaded with them.

"Nicole, we simply aren't taking *no* for an answer. You can either walk out of here with us, or we'll get the guys to come and drag you out, but you're going out for a day of much-needed pampering," Trinity said.

"Go with them, Nicole. You've been amazing, and I love you more than anything, but you need to take care of yourself and not just me all the time. Now get out of here, and I'll tell the doctors you aren't allowed back in until tomorrow," Patsy told her.

"Patsy, you don't mean that. You need me here," Nicole said, a little hurt by her sister's words.

"I do need you, but I know how much you sacrifice and how much you've always given up for me. Get the shocked look off your face. I'm not blind. You make sacrifices every day to take care of me, and I love and appreciate you even more for that, but please take care of yourself. Now get out, and I mean it when I say you aren't allowed back until tomorrow," Patsy reinforced.

"You're never a sacrifice because I love you," Nicole told her.

"You heard your sister. Let's get out of here," Jasmine said.

"I guess it wouldn't hurt to get out for a few hours," Nicole conceded. Both women nodded encouragingly. She gathered her purse and made sure Patsy was properly covered before reluctantly following the women from the room.

"First thing we are doing is getting you a hot lunch," Trinity said.

"Then we're going to the salon for manicures and pedicures," Jasmine added.

"After all that fun, we're doing some shopping, and don't you dare shake your head at me. It looks as if you haven't pampered yourself

97

in a long time. I've demanded Ryan's credit card, so your day's on him. Seriously, you've got to quit shaking your head at me. The man isn't going to go broke because you purchase a few outfits," Trinity said.

Nicole was thinking there was no way she was going to spend Ryan's money. He'd already forked out an arm and a leg on Patsy's operation, but she could live with that because it wasn't for her. She didn't find it acceptable to have him buying her personal clothing, though.

"We can argue about it more once you're fed and pampered. Then I'll feel better winning because my opponent doesn't look like she's about to blow over in a small wind," Jasmine said with a smile.

The three women ate an amazing lunch, which had Nicole groaning and wishing she could unbutton her jeans. On the way to the salon, she realized that she'd never had either a pedicure or manicure, and the thought of that luxury was out of this world. She sat back in the plush chair while a woman rubbed lotion over her feet, and she knew in that moment that she'd died and gone to heaven. If there was a greater pleasure in life, she wasn't sure what it was.

"Okay. That was a slice of heaven. Now let's do some shopping," Trinity said with a pleased look on her face.

"Seriously, the lunch and the salon were amazing, and I really am feeling much better. Ryan and I have just started seeing each other, and I'm not comfortable with him buying me clothes," Nicole told them. She couldn't tell them she was basically selling herself to the man for her sister's operation.

"Nicole, we can do this the easy way or the hard way," Jasmine once again threatened.

"Why don't we wander around, and I can be with you guys while you get new things," Nicole tried to compromise. The two women smiled at each other and dragged her off toward some fancy store.

Nicole ran her hands along the silk of some gowns and knew it was all beyond her normal price range. She wouldn't even be able to afford a pair of panties in a store like the one the girls had brought her to. When Patsy graduated and she was able to get some more education, maybe Nicole would be able to spoil herself a bit, but that would be several years into the future. She really didn't mind the menial sacrifices, though, as long as her sister turned out okay. It would be a miracle, considering the parents they were unfortunate enough to have received.

"Derek and I are throwing a masquerade ball, and you need a stunning gown for it," Jasmine told her.

"I probably shouldn't go to a party and leave Patsy, anyway," Nicole said with reluctance. The thought of going to a large party was very appealing, especially all dressed up. It would be really nice to feel like a princess for a night, but she couldn't justify spending the funds.

"Patsy will be well taken care of, and it would truly hurt my feelings if you didn't come," Jasmine said, sealing Nicole's fate. She wouldn't want to hurt either of the two women who'd been so good to her.

"Okay, I guess it wouldn't hurt to get one dress, but seriously, it doesn't have to be extravagant," Nicole conceded. Both Jasmine and

Trinity squealed with delight and, by the end of their shopping day, Nicole was regretting those few simple words.

She didn't know how the women had managed it, but she ended up walking from the stores with several bags and the most stunning dress she'd ever seen. She'd felt amazing when she tried it on. She couldn't imagine how she was going to feel when her hair was all done and she had on the heels and accessories. She was looking forward to the masquerade, but she was terrified to know how much she'd spent. She was determined to pay every cent back.

Trinity and Jasmine refused to let her see any of the totals, but she'd tell Ryan she wanted to know the amount and she'd pay him back. She wouldn't allow him to refuse her. She felt too much like a call girl, with him buying her clothes.

"I'll take your dress and accessories back to my place. I want you to come over early so we can all get ready together," Jasmine told her. She'd still not let her see what she'd bought to go with the dress.

"That would be nice," Nicole told her. By the time they headed back to the hospital, Nicole realized she'd had an amazing day, but she was certainly exhausted. The women left her, and she quickly fell asleep in the cot the staff had brought in for her.

It was her first night of sleeping soundly, through the whole night, since the surgery. She was grateful Patsy had been sound asleep herself, or she figured her little sister would've carried through on her threat and made her leave until the morning. Nicole would've been too stressed to sleep at the house. Besides, she was trying to avoid Ryan. She really didn't think she'd be able to resist him.

"I'm fine. You can really stop fussing over me now," Patsy said, impatient with her overprotective sister.

"I'm simply worried about you. You did have major surgery, and are finally safe and sound and out of that horrible hospital," Nicole told her little sister with all the patience of a saint. Patsy had been in a dreadful mood the last few days and was incredibly sick of lying in bed. She'd always been an active child, and she was thoroughly sick of bed rest.

"Remember, your doctor said you can't overdo it--only mild walks, and no school for at least another month," Nicole reminded her.

"Trust me. I have you here to remind me," Patsy told her with a sincere smile.

"I love you so much," Nicole told her, fighting back the tears.

"I love you too, sis. Now go relax for a while. I promise you I won't melt away while I sit here and watch a movie," Patsy told her. "I can't believe we are in this amazing house, and I really hope we get to stay for a while," she added.

Patsy had been just as amazed at Ryan's home as Nicole had initially been. She'd been staying there for a little over two weeks now and had adjusted to the palatial place. For Patsy, it was all brand new, and she wanted to explore everything. She was still getting winded too easily, though, and she had to take it easy. Nicole was going to make sure she did indeed relax.

"What is it?" Ryan snapped at his poor receptionist when she buzzed him.

"I'm sorry to interrupt you, Mr. Titan, but you have a call on line one," she said. His entire office staff had gone out of their way to avoid him over the last two weeks. He'd been a bear to be around, and he couldn't seem to stop himself.

Nicole had been living with him for a couple weeks, and he hadn't been alone with her since the night her sister had gone in for surgery. She'd stayed night and day at the hospital and, though he'd wanted to drag her from the room by her hair and insist she share his bed, he couldn't do it.

He convinced himself he was only thinking about Patsy and didn't care about what Nicole had actually needed. Even though he wanted his revenge on her, he couldn't hurt her as badly as he would've been if he'd made her leave her sister. Nicole had only started to look better in the last few days. She was finally sleeping, and her skin was getting a healthy flush to it. It would feel much better to challenge her if she was able to give as well as she got.

Patsy had finally been moved to Ryan's house that afternoon, and Nicole would be back in his bed tonight. Maybe after he'd satisfied his needs, he'd stop snapping at every person who dared to even look at him.

"Thanks," he said shortly and took the call. He barely managed to be civil to the man on the other end of the line and wouldn't be surprised if he didn't call back for a very long time. Ryan gave up on work and headed out the door. He was in no state to be around decent people.

His driver got him home in record time, since there wasn't any rush hour traffic to deal with. He slipped inside and worked the rest of the day from his home office. He didn't trust himself to be around Nicole yet because he was sure she was tending her sister, and it wouldn't be good for Patsy's heart to watch her sister be ravished right in front of her. Man, he was acting like a horny teenager.

His door opened, and he was about to growl at the person who dared to interrupt him, when

Derek stepped in through the door. He still grumbled a bit, even at his cousin.

"What's up your burr?" Derek asked with a laugh.

Ryan ignored the question. "What do you want, Derek?" he asked. He knew he was being rude, but this arrangement with Nicole was seriously killing him. He was supposed to have her in his bed every night, and so far all he'd gotten was one night in two weeks.

"I was just coming to remind you about the party tomorrow night," Derek said, barely able to suppress his humor at his cousin's mood.

"I did forget about that. I don't know if I can make it with Patsy just getting here," Ryan said. He was certainly in no mood to be at a party, and he was sure he wouldn't be able to drag Nicole away.

"Well that's too bad because then you're going to miss out on Nicole looking hot and sexy," Derek said, knowing he'd get a reaction from his cousin.

Ryan's head flew up in surprise. "I didn't think she'd be willing to part from her sister, even though I hired 'round the clock care for her," he grumbled.

"She's already at the house. Jasmine insisted she and Trinity stay the night so they could do the whole beauty thing together," Derek said with a shrug.

"Crap. I feel out of the loop. I didn't even know she'd left. She and I are going to have a serious talk," Ryan said, a bit of a threat in his tone.

"Sounds as if you're being knocked off your feet by a woman," Derek told him, with far too smug a look on his face. Ryan simply glared at him until Derek chuckled. He then went over and helped himself to a generous amount of Ryan's best bourbon.

"Well, Drew is on his way over. We figured, if the girls were kicking us out, then we would make it a guy's night," Derek told him. "So put your work away, and let's go out to the grease joint."

"Sounds good to me," Ryan agreed. Drew showed up, and the men headed out. Being with his cousins helped his mood slightly, but Ryan knew he wasn't going to feel better until he had

Nicole back in his bed again. He couldn't wait
until he got her out of his system for good.

CHAPTER FIVE

"So, I know it's completely over the top, but we have a hair stylist and a make-up artist coming in tomorrow. I want to wow my husband, and I have spared no expense," Jasmine said with a giggle.

Nicole's eyes widened at the amount of money this family seemed to have. She couldn't imagine ever being comfortable having someone hired to come in and do her hair and make-up. That was for movie stars and models, of which she was neither. She felt way in over her head.

"I've got all the beauty products we need for tonight. It's a good thing you sent your husband away; otherwise, he'd go screaming from the house," Trinity said as she produced a large bag and emptied the contents onto the kitchen table.

Nicole picked up a few of the products, having no clue what they were for. There were facial masks, lotions, essential oils and body scrubs. She had the feeling her body was going to be completely raw come morning.

"Let's head up to my room to apply the masks. We can do the paraffin wax on our hands and feet next. After that, we'll take baths and turn our skin to silk," Jasmine said, as she quickly started putting all the things back in the bag. The two women dragged Nicole up the stairs for their night of beauty to begin.

Nicole had never had such an amazing night, and she never wanted it to end. After several hours of beauty treatments, her skin felt like smooth satin, and her face was still tingling from whatever they'd plastered all over her. She felt attractive and mellow, and she was incredibly nervous about the next day.

The women didn't get to sleep until after two in the morning, but they slept until noon. It was a luxury Nicole had never before allowed herself. When she awoke, the day began in earnest, and she was plucked and waxed and twisted in every imaginable way.

She was now standing before a full-length mirror and didn't recognize the person staring back at her. The dress was stunning and showed off every one of her curves to perfection, and the accessories Jasmine and Trinity had added were over the top. She really felt like a princess about to enter her first ball. Jasmine had insisted on her borrowing some jewelry, and Nicole was terrified one of the huge sapphires was going to fall from her ears. She didn't want to even think about the cost of them.

"You're the most stunning creature ever. When Ryan sees you tonight, he's going to have a heart attack. Beyond that, every man in the room will be determined to whisk you away from him. I can't wait to see his face," Trinity said, coming up to stand beside her.

Nicole thought she was the one who was stunning. Both Trinity and Jasmine were beyond gorgeous in their gowns and jewelry. No one would ever be able to guess they'd both had children because it certainly didn't show in their perfect figures. Nicole never would've realized she was equally as devastating.

When the women finally made their entrance into the hall, wearing their jeweled masks, every head in the place turned to watch. The women could hear the three cousins sucking in air, which wasn't released for some time, at their entrance

Nicole looked around the huge room and wondered how the women had talked her into going to the party. She wanted to turn around and leave the instant she saw all the fancily dressed people filling up the place, all wearing masks. She was so out of her league.

Jasmine and Trinity were whisked away by their husbands, leaving Nicole standing there, feeling foolish. Ryan wasn't approaching her, which she figured was most likely a good thing, but she was also too insecure to handle being all alone.

She had just turned to leave when someone tugged on her arm. "Is that you, Nicole?" a woman asked her.

"Yes," she answered. Nicole couldn't figure out who was speaking to her. The masks certainly hid one's identity, but she should still be able to have an inkling of who the person was.

"It's Stephanie. We went to school together, remember?" she said, and Nicole then knew exactly who it was. They'd been friends for years but, like everyone else she'd once been close to, she'd lost contact.

"It's so great to see you, Stephanie. It's been too many years," Nicole said, truly meaning her words. It was nice to see another familiar face in a crowd of strangers.

Stephanie gave her a hug. "Don't let this party intimidate you. Jasmine would never invite anyone who was too horrible," Stephanie reassured her.

"I know, but I feel too old to be at a dance," Nicole told her self-consciously.

"Seriously, you need to live a little bit--once in a while--is my philosophy. I remember, from school, you were far more likely to study than to attend a dance, so let go and pretend you have no responsibilities for a night. Most people won't even recognize you, and you look beyond gorgeous, so stop worrying about things and allow yourself to have a great time," Stephanie told her.

Nicole knew Stephanie was right. What made anyone else in the room any better than her? Ryan had insisted she hang on his arm at certain events like arm candy, so she'd better get used to it. Besides, just because the other people in the room were blessed with more money than they needed, didn't make them any better than her.

A lot of the people were from money and hadn't worked an honest day in their lives. She didn't mean Jasmine and Derek. They were the nicest people she'd ever known. She could see from the looks of some of the guests, though, that it was all about who had the most expensive things, and that was a huge turn off for Nicole.

"I'm off to find some sexy man to whisk me to paradise," Stephanie told her. "I'll look for you later. It really was great to see you," she added and hugged Nicole.

Stephanie took off in one direction and left Nicole to wander around to a quiet corner. She grabbed a plate and swiped some food. She was starving, and the smells from the food were making her stomach growl. She was used to eating Top Ramen, or a good soup when she was really lucky, so the table full of delicacies was making her practically drool.

She was still living each day as if she was on her last meal. It was how it had been for too many years to remember anything different. She loaded her plate to overflowing, and then snuck off to a corner to start shoveling it in, praying no one noticed her. She was certainly not acting like any of the other women who'd never eat at a function, in fear of gaining a pound or getting something stuck between their teeth.

###

Ryan was standing in a group of people, desperately trying to keep up with the boring conversation, but his eyes were following Nicole everywhere she went. He was trying to maintain some distance from her, but the second he'd spotted her in the figure hugging gown, his groin had jumped to life, and he'd known he was far better off to avoid her for a while. He certainly approved of whatever the girls had been up to the night before.

He half-listened to what his companions were talking about. He nodded where he was supposed to and uttered a comment here and there, but his eyes never left Nicole. He felt his lips tilt, as he noticed her flick her eyes around the room guiltily, and then fill her plate to overflowing. If he had any doubts she wasn't one of the high society women normally at the parties, her full plate would've clued him in. He was thinking he was going to play a game with her that night.

Why not start from scratch and pretend to be strangers? He could romance her and add some mystery to their relationship. Nothing else seemed to be working to keep her mind off her worries, so why not spice things up?, he thought. He was getting more excited by the moment, imagining how things were going to end that night.

Ryan watched as she glanced around again and seemed to sigh a bit as she didn't think anyone was watching her.

He couldn't believe he'd almost refused to come to the masquerade. His mood lightened considerably. As he looked around, he noticed all the women wearing their usual skimpy designer dresses and ostentatious jewelry.

Even though it was a masquerade, and everyone was supposed to disguise themselves, the women wanted to be noticed, and most held masques on sticks, so they could move them aside. He was personally wearing a Zorro mask, but it hadn't taken the barracuda women long to figure out who he was, and they were swarming him. They would be shocked to find who he chose to take home with him. Most of the people in the room knew nothing of his past.

"Ryan, you didn't hear a word I just said," the grating voice of the current female trying to hold his attention said. She'd been giving him signals for months she was readily available and looking for her next husband to keep her in the lifestyle to which she was so accustomed. He hadn't wanted to be rude, but he had a feeling he was going to have to spell it out in black and white that he wasn't interested.

"I'm sorry. My mind was on business," he easily lied, soothing her feelings. She gave her best fake smile and rubbed her barely-covered breasts up against his arm. He felt nothing from the touch. "I'm sorry to leave you ladies, but I'm going for a bite to eat, then I have business to discuss with Tom," he said, as he pulled away from the group.

"You know how to find us when you're ready to play instead of talk business," another woman pouted at him. He couldn't even remember her name. He needed to make it known soon he was no longer available, although he knew that wouldn't stop most of the women he was used to dealing with. He walked away and forgot all about them as soon as he left.

He kept his eyes on Nicole, feeling a clenching in his gut as he tried to figure out what she was thinking of the party. He knew it was so far removed from her normal life she was most likely uncomfortable.

He was stopped several times on his way over toward her and had to fight to not growl at the continued interruptions. He wanted to get to her before she decided to slip away. He wouldn't be able to play out his game if she were to run away and change. After all, it was a masquerade. The night was about secrets and romance.

He ignored the next couple of people who tried to stop him and made a beeline toward Nicole. Damn, she was so unlike the stick figure women surrounding him. She had on a fitted black dress, showing off her luscious hips and impressive breasts to perfection. Her stomach was flat, and her legs seemed to go on forever. She was wearing a pair of high heels that only enhanced those gorgeous legs. He'd definitely make sure his cousins' spouses took her shopping more often, since he liked the effect.

He wanted to see her dark hair released from the bun it was currently tied in. He wanted to rip the mask off her features and see her flawless skin,

119

but then the mystery of the game would fade away.

"How are you this evening?" he asked from behind her, as he finally made his way to her darkened corner. He had to fight the smile as her entire body stiffened for a moment as she slowly turned to face him. He felt another clench in his gut as she looked at him with her incredible blue eyes enhanced by makeup to look even more exotic than ever before. The part of her face he could see was stunning, as usual. *Let the games begin.*

Nicole looked at Ryan and forgot how to speak for a moment. He was seriously the sexiest guy she'd ever encountered before, even with the mask — or maybe because of it. He towered over her own five-and-a-half foot height, making her have to look upward. He had broad shoulders, shown to perfection beneath the custom made black suit.

He'd been gorgeous as a teenager, but the man before her was simply breathtaking.

His full lips were tilted up in a smile that seemed to be hiding some kind of a secret. His intense green eyes were looking at her as if she was his next conquest, and she found the idea wasn't unpleasant. She saw his hand lifting toward her mask and quickly took a step backwards.

"I'm wonderful, and yourself?" she finally managed to answer him, with what she hoped was the proper amount of mystery.

"I'm much better now that I've managed to find you. Have we met before?" he asked.

She couldn't figure out what he was playing at, but she found she was intrigued. She knew he had no doubts about who she was but, for some reason, he wanted to play a game. She was willing to play along for a while, especially after her glass of champagne. She also had added confidence from her clothes and expertly applied make-up.

"I believe I'd remember meeting you, but isn't the whole point of a masquerade to remain a mystery?" she asked. She was surprised by the quivering in her stomach, which didn't seem to be subsiding. She had to admit she was still attracted to Ryan, and his admiration was stroking her ego.

"Ah, yes. A masquerade is full of mystery, but I'm finding I really want to see what's behind your mask," he said, putting his full amount of charm behind the words.

"Haven't you heard you don't always get what you want?" she said with a full smile. She knew she needed to make an excuse and get away from him, but she found she was enjoying the flirting. What could it harm, anyway? She could put all their problems behind her for one night. He wouldn't try anything at the party, and she could go back to being distant when the bell chimed midnight. For now, though, she felt like Cinderella, which made her daring and bold.

"Actually, no one has told me *no* for about twelve years," he answered. He smiled at the thought.

"Well then, I think it's about time you were told you can't have something you want," she said with a seductive smile. She then turned and started to walk away, but Ryan quickly caught up to her at the edge of the dance floor. Without saying a word, he pulled her into his arms.Nicole had turned down many dates in her life, and the men seemed to crawl away with their tail between their legs. She'd never walked away before and had the guy chase after her. She found she was incredibly turned on by his boldness. That worried her more than anything else. The game was suddenly starting to scare her. She should've known she could never compete with a man like Ryan. He was far out of her league. She kept her body stiff, as his hand pushed on her lower back, pulling her into his strength.

"I don't recall you asking me to dance, and I certainly didn't say I would," she finally said as she stood stock-still in his arms.

"I didn't ask," he said with confidence, as he looked down into her eyes. "We're starting to make a scene, so unless you like to be the center of attention, I suggest you simply go with the dance because I'm not letting go."

Nicole thought about stomping on his foot with the high heel of her shoe, but she noticed several heads were turned their way and didn't want anyone to notice her. If anyone really took a look at her, they'd realize quickly that she didn't belong in their world. She glared up at him as she allowed him to maneuver her around the dance floor. He kept pulling her tightly against his body, and she kept pushing away from it. It was a game they played for the next several minutes.

Ryan swept his hand lower over her well-rounded hips, and Nicole quickly reached around and pushed it back up. It was a game of cat and mouse, and she felt that he was gaining the victory. She glared at him, even as she felt her pulse accelerating. She could tell by the look on his face that he could feel it too. Her eyes darkened with desire and her breath started coming out in pants against his neck. She was as turned on as he was, but she was doing her best to fight it.

"I'm a little too warm. I need to step outside," she said. She was frustrated with herself at the breathless quality in her tone. How was she going to convince Ryan she didn't want him when she couldn't control her own desire, which contradicted her words? She knew they had an agreement, but that didn't mean she had to be so easy.

"I could use a cooling off myself," he said between clenched teeth.

Nicole said nothing else as she pulled away from him and started walking to the balcony doors. She tried to pull her hand free, but he refused to let go. She couldn't pull free of his touch without attracting attention, so she once again let him have his way. She was going to give him a piece of her mind if he didn't back off, though.

They stepped through the doorway onto the dark balcony. Ryan looked over his shoulder before closing the door and uttered a sigh of relief. He released Nicole's hand, and she quickly went to the far end of the balcony, trying to get as far from him as possible.

Ryan quietly grabbed a deck chair and pushed it under the doorknob. He didn't want anyone coming out and interrupting his time with her. It had been too long since he'd been deep inside her body, and no one was going to stop him that night.

Nicole leaned against the railing and tried to get her body back under control. She was playing a game with a man who could eat her for lunch. He'd been the one in control from the moment she made that phone call, and he was once again letting her know it. She could feel her breathing slowly get back under control and her heartbeat returning to a normal rate. She continued to stare out at the nearly black sky.

In Seattle, a clear night was a rare thing, and that night was no exception. It was unusually warm, but the cloud cover sealed the deck off completely from the rest of the world. She'd gain control over her raging hormones and slip back inside and away from the party she should've never attended in the first place. She should be helping her sister, not flirting with the man who was making her into something she despised.

As Nicole was getting ready to turn back around, she felt Ryan come up behind her, his hands wrapping around her body. Her pulse skyrocketed, and her breathing exercises went out the window. One touch from him, and she felt like a bowl of Jell-O, with zero control over her own body.

His hands were splayed across her stomach, and his body was pressed along the length of her back. She could feel his hot breath on her neck and couldn't stop the shiver running down her spine. He said nothing as he stood there and rubbed circles on her quivering stomach.

"I really need to get back and check on Patsy," she said, barely above a whisper.

"She has 'round the clock care, so what's your hurry?" he asked before she felt the press of his lips on her neck. She was barely able to contain the groan wanting to escape her throat. His mouth felt so good touching her skin. He was kissing along the length of her neck, and she could feel the swipe of his tongue along her beating pulse point. She'd stop him in just a moment. He'd asked her a question but, for the life of her, she couldn't remember what it was.

His hands continued to caress her stomach, causing her body to shake with need. She was quickly losing her resolve to walk away. What would it hurt to have one night of recklessness?

She'd always been the good girl, the responsible one, the one who could be counted on. She'd always walked away to make a better choice. Their making love again was inevitable, so why keep fighting it?

"Tell me you want me," he demanded. His hands skimmed higher, and she could feel the brush of them on the underside of her breasts, which were swollen and aching to feel his masculine hands grip them. Her nipples were straining against her bra, and the lace was irritating her sensitive skin. She'd never wanted her clothing off so badly. She'd never wanted a man to touch her more than she wanted her next breath of oxygen.

"No," she finally managed to choke out. He seemed to tense for a moment before he growled low in his throat and bit the side of her neck. She felt a slight sting and then unbelievable pleasure as he ran his tongue over the spot and then sucked it into his mouth.

His hands finally pushed over the mounds of her breasts, and she gasped as his thumbs rubbed over her tightened nipples. He rubbed his hips into her backside, and she could feel his erection pushing into her. She couldn't stop herself from pressing her body back into his. His growl of pleasure gave her a boldness she didn't know she possessed.

He quickly turned her around, molding his mouth over hers, and all other thoughts were wiped from her mind. When his tongue slipped inside, she saw an explosion of light behind her eyelids.

She wrapped her arms around his neck and clung to him as his hands roamed all over her body. She didn't know how, or when, it happened, but suddenly she felt the warm breeze on her naked breasts a few seconds before she felt his mouth break from hers, only to take her swollen bud into his mouth.

She threw her head back as he lavished her aching breasts. He took his time on one before switching to the other to give it equal attention. She could feel the heat pooling in her core and wanted nothing more than for him to fill the void inside her.

His hands were rubbing along her thighs, and she wanted more. She needed him in a way she'd never needed a man before. He was turning her into an addict for his body. The things he did to her were almost worth the guilt when it was over.

Ryan pulled her dress up and groaned aloud at the wisp of fabric covering her core. She was suddenly grateful Jasmine had made her purchase the sexy lingerie.

###

His hand brushed over the fabric, and he lost all sense of control when he felt the wetness soaking the thin material. She was the most responsive woman he'd ever been with, and there was nothing fake about her. She was all woman, and she was writhing in pleasure beneath his touch. It was quickly sending him over the edge. He grabbed the side of her thong, and it easily ripped in his hand and left her uncovered for his pleasure. He'd never wanted light more in his life than at that moment. He could barely see her body, and he wanted to take in every inch of her.

He grabbed her in his arms and laid her down in one of the loungers on the deck. He buried his head in the juncture between her thighs and, as her sweet scent hit him, he felt his body pulse in painful desire. She was so beautiful, and the groans coming from her were making him realize he wasn't going to last long. He wanted to draw it out, but there would be next time for that.

Nicole jerked in pleasure at the first swipe of his tongue against her aroused flesh. She'd never felt so out of control and couldn't stop moving under his masterful administrations to her sensitive body. He swiped his tongue along her moist folds and took the sensitized bud into his mouth, gently sucking it. That was all it took to send her flying over a cliff which seemed to have no bottom. Her body jerked in a powerful orgasm as wave after wave of ecstasy washed through her. She was shaking as the pleasure rushed through her in what seemed like an endless storm.

She felt his finger dip inside of her heat and wanted to shake her head *no*. She couldn't take any more lovemaking. Her body was spent, and she could barely breathe as it was. His tongue traveled the length of her body upwards until his lips fastened onto her still-sensitive nipples once again. She felt a stirring in her stomach as he took the still-hardened peaks into his mouth and sucked them deep inside. When he gently bit down on her, her back arched off the lounger, and she felt the stirrings of pleasure start to rise again.

She'd heard about women who could have more than one orgasm during a single love-making session, but she'd never thought she could be so sexual. Her eyes widened in shock as she felt the heat building to an unbearable pitch again. His fingers were still inside her, slowly pumping in and out of her heated folds, and she once again started to wiggle beneath his administering. He moved his body upwards, and suddenly his lips were fastened onto hers.

He thrust his tongue inside of her mouth, giving as much as he took. He moved his hand from her body, and she cried out at the empty feeling. She needed more, but she didn't even know what that need was. "Please," she cried out, not knowing what she was crying out for.

She felt the weight of his body as he settled over her thighs. He was gloriously naked above her, and she greedily rubbed her hands along the muscled length of his back and arms. He was kissing her so deeply she could barely breathe, but she didn't care. She didn't need oxygen. She didn't need anything but the feeling he was bringing her. She suddenly felt pressure as he pushed up against her opening and a new wave of heat hit her, moistening her body for his entrance.

He lifted his lips from hers and bit gently down on her neck again as he thrust inside her in one long motion. She tensed up from the sheer size of the man. She knew it would be a long time before she could take him inside her without feeling stretched beyond her limits. Her body took him in and, as she adjusted around him, the pleasure was almost too much to bear. She heard him swear as he tried to gain some control of himself. She felt him start to pull out of her, but she was finally adjusting to his size, and she wanted him to move within her, not leave her empty.

Ryan could feel he'd stretched her too much. He was too big for her and needed to get some control over himself. How could he forget the sight of his sheets the last time? Then she wrapped her legs around his back and jerked her hips upwards, and he lost all sense of control. With her thrust upwards, he was sent over the edge, and there was no going back.

###

Nicole could feel the sheen of sweat from both their bodies, allowing them to easily rub against each other. As he grabbed her hips and started thrusting in and out of her, faster and faster, she was quickly building up to a crashing crescendo. Her nipples were rubbing up against his hard chest, and every time he sank deep inside of her, her swollen nub would brush against his pelvic bone. Between all the sensations he was giving her, she could feel the orgasm getting ready to take her away. She held onto him and didn't even think about fighting it.

He was pushing into her harder and harder, and suddenly she couldn't take any more. Her body tensed as the most earth-shattering explosion washed through her. She shook as wave after wave of electricity shot through her body. Her legs were in a death grip around his back, and her nails dug into his shoulders. The release washed through her, over and over again, and she couldn't prevent the cry that rang from her scorched throat.

###

Ryan was barely hanging on to his sanity as he pushed deep inside of her, and when she started gripping him, he was completely lost. He let his own cry of pleasure ring out as he emptied himself deep inside of her. She was the most passionate woman he'd ever taken, and he didn't want it to end, but how could he not want to feel total completion? It was unlike anything else he'd ever experienced. She continued to grip him in convulsions, draining him of every last ounce of himself. He fell against her in satisfaction, and then shifted them to their sides.

His body was burning up, and he was grateful for the gentle breeze blowing against them. He couldn't open his eyes as he lay there with her in his arms. He stroked her back, and neither of them said anything. They could always talk later.

CHAPTER SIX

Nicole woke up because she was freezing. She started to panic as she wondered where she was. As she moved and felt arms around her, everything came back to her with the force of a wrecking crane.

She couldn't believe how easily she'd fallen into his arms once again. She was never going to convince the man he didn't want to be in a relationship with her when she continued to fall into bed with him the second he touched her. Her entire goal was for him to get sick of her so she and Patsy could get on with their lives. She was already starting to have deep feelings for him again, and that would never do. He was simply with her to exact some kind of revenge for the way she'd left him. He couldn't know she'd done it for the best possible reasons.

Nicole slowly began to untangle herself from his arms. He started to stir, and she went completely still. She wanted nothing more than to get as far from him as she could and figure out what she was going to do next. She knew he'd be angry with her, as he'd told her she wouldn't run from his bed again, but that was one thing in her control, and she couldn't let it go. Besides, she wasn't technically in a bed, so she wasn't breaking any of his ridiculous rules.

She finally managed to untangle herself from his arms and searched the darkened deck for her missing clothes. Luckily, the dress never came off all the way, and her light jacket was easy to find. She couldn't spot her panties and decided she didn't care.

She walked toward the doors and spotted the deck chair under the doorknob. She was both horrified and relieved to see it. She was glad no one had been able to come out and spot her lying in his arms, half-naked, and yet she was horrified that he'd thought to enclose the two of them. He must've had zero doubts she'd succumb to him once again.

She was trying to decide how to remove the chair, without making any noise, when she spotted a staircase to her left. She walked over and was relieved to see it led to the yard below. She knew the walk back to his house was a long one, but there was a trail, and it would be good for her. She'd have plenty of time to think about what she was going to do next.

Ryan woke up a while after Nicole slipped away and looked around in disbelief. He couldn't believe she'd once again run out on him. He'd told her she wasn't to leave his bed. He had to smile to himself mockingly, considering she didn't really break his rule, as they'd fallen asleep in a lounger. He jumped up and straightened his clothing. The sun was just starting to come up in the sky, giving him a bit of light.

He spotted her delicate panties, which were completely destroyed. He threw them in his pocket. Then he looked over the deck. There was no sign of her anywhere. He saw the chair was still under the doorknob, so he knew she must've escaped down the stairs.

He squared his shoulders and headed toward his vehicle. There was no way he wanted to risk running into his cousin, with his knowing eyes. He wouldn't live it down that his woman snuck off in the middle of the night. Hell, Derek and Drew were both incredibly lucky men. They had beautiful wives who idolized them. Their women were in no way pushovers and had certainly given his cousins a run for their money. But he knew they didn't slip from their beds in the middle of the night. No, his cousins most likely woke up to be satisfied fully each morning, instead of left aching.

Luckily, there was no one about at this early hour of the morning, and he was able to sneak off. He headed straight for home, where he planned on having a rip-roaring fight with her, and she'd certainly learn her place. He was going to teach her that her place was in his bed. He cringed a bit at how chauvinistic he sounded, but he didn't care. She was his, and she needed to learn that.

Ryan wasn't normally a man who ever accepted defeat, which was why he had billions in his bank account. She'd soon learn this fact. He pulled into his driveway in anticipation. He slowed the car as he drove up the long driveway. He could take his time now because he knew soon he'd get what he wanted.

He stepped through the front doors, and all was quiet in the house. He peeked in on Patsy, who was sleeping soundly. He smiled at her much healthier complexion, knowing she was going to be okay. That alone was worth all the heartache her sister was giving him.

He climbed the stairs and, of course, she wasn't in his room. He blew out a breath of frustration. He next went to the room he'd found her in the last time and opened the door. His breath was knocked out of him. Standing before him was Nicole in nothing but a towel. She was so unbelievably gorgeous, even without a lick of makeup on her face and her hair hanging wetly down her back.

She glared at him, and he glared right back. It was time to let her know how a proper mistress acted. She seemed to have forgotten in the last couple of weeks.

"I woke up alone again," he stated the obvious.

"And this concerns me how?" she asked with a raise of her brows.

Her snide answer sent his blood to boiling. "I told you that you won't leave my bed in the middle of the night," he growled at her.

"And I told you I'll do as I please," she snapped right back. He slowly began to stalk toward her, and he was satisfied when her eyes rounded and she started to retreat from him.

"Are you trying to break our agreement, Nicole?" he asked quietly.

"You don't own me," she whispered.

"Oh, but I do own you, Nicole. Our agreement is I help your sister, and you're my mistress until I see fit to dispose of you. You aren't keeping me very happy right now, so I guess I could throw you and Patsy out of here. Then she wouldn't get the medical treatment she still needs," he threatened her. He knew he was sinking to an all-time low, but he was so angry he didn't even care.

"You wouldn't do that," she said, but her voice didn't hold much confidence.

"Try me. Leave my bed again before I'm ready for you to, and you'll see exactly what I'll do," he said with a confident smile. He prayed she wouldn't call his bluff because there was no way in hell he'd punish Patsy. His ace in the hole was that Nicole had no idea what he would or wouldn't do.

"I hate you," she spat at him. He smiled hugely at her, as his gaze flicked over her body. She was flushed, and her breathing was coming out in pants. She may hate him, but her body wanted him and she couldn't deny that.

"You sure haven't acted like you hate me when you're moaning in my arms," he said with confidence.

"How can you be so sure I'm not faking the whole thing?" she said with her own version of a cocky smile. She wasn't pulling it off. His eyes narrowed even further, and he stalked closer to her. He now had her backed up to the bed, with nowhere to go. He was breathing just as heavily as her, and his temper was close to the snapping point.

He ran his hand along the top of the towel, making her body shiver, betraying her words. He smiled in triumph once again, and she continued to glare at him. She'd thrown down her bluff, and he'd won. It was definitely a heady feeling.

"Deny it all you want, but you want me just as badly as I want you. You can play the martyr, but we both know sharing my bed is no hardship for you," he said as he continued to caress her skin.

She said nothing else. Ryan knew she'd lost the small battle, but she wouldn't concede the entire war. She tilted her chin in defiance, which only made him smile more. He grabbed the knot on her towel and, in one movement, ripped the thing off of her, leaving her completely naked in front of him.

Nicole gasped aloud at his boldness, and he saw in her face that she badly wanted to cover herself up. She had to feel exposed, standing before him completely naked. There was no way to hide his effect on her, with her nipples already hardened into tight peaks.

Ryan felt like he'd been kicked in the gut at the sight of her luscious curves before him, and he was no longer angry. He was hungry, and he was going to prove how much she needed him. He did exactly that over the next several hours and felt immense satisfaction as she lay in his arms, sound asleep afterward.

He was too wired to fall asleep and slowly untangled himself from her. He felt much better and decided to get some work done. He'd proven his point, and though he knew she'd still fight him each step of the way, he didn't think he'd wake up to find her in another bed again.

He realized he'd always been surrounded by women willing to concede to him with the slightest crook of his finger, but that bored him. He was glad she was stubborn and independent. She certainly wouldn't bore him. He actually whistled as he took his shower and dressed for the day. Then he headed downstairs. The drive to the office didn't take him long.

He almost laughed aloud at the relieved looks on his staff members' faces as he smiled and asked how their day was going. He hadn't realized what a complete grouch he'd been. He had a feeling his mood was only going to improve each day he had with Nicole. He pushed the button to page his secretary.

"Can you please get Nicole on the line and put her through?"

"Yes sir," she efficiently replied. He could've easily rung her himself, especially since he was sitting at his desk doing nothing in anticipation of her voice coming over the line, but this was a game of who had the most power, and he was determined to win.

"She's on line three, sir," the voice spoke over his intercom. He forced himself to wait a full two minutes before picking up the phone.

"Hello, Ryan here," he spoke into the handset as if bored.

"You're the one who called me," she said, sounding exasperated.

"Oh, yes. I almost forgot," Ryan lied. "I'd like for you to come into the office today and have lunch with me," he told her.

"I'm busy," she said simply, and his easy mood evaporated.

"Well, then you'll undo any plans you've made and be here by noon," he told her, brooking no room for argument. The other end of the line was silent for so long he was beginning to think she'd actually had the audacity to hang up on him. His good mood was gone, and he was about to explode.

"Fine. I'll be there," she finally said in a none-too-happy voice.

"Good. I'll see you then," he practically yelled before disconnecting the call. He was seething mad as he sat in his chair. There were women all

147

around who'd be climbing all over themselves to spend one minute in his company, and the one woman he actually wanted to be with acted as if she was going to the gallows every time he requested her presence. It was absolutely ridiculous, and he needed to gain some control over himself. He refused to let her affect him so much.

"Mr. Titan, you have an international call on line one," his secretary's voice came over the intercom.

"I've got it," he snapped at the woman. He received no reply, and rightfully so. His staff was terrified of what kind of a mood he'd be in because it changed every two minutes. He took the call and was grateful it occupied him over the next couple of hours. He didn't have time to sit around and brood about what Nicole was thinking or doing.

He was working on one of his accounts when his door opened. He was surprised, since no one ever walked into his office without either calling first, or at least knocking. He was about to bite the intruder's head off for having the gall to interrupt him in his current mood when Nicole flowed through the doorway.

"Has no one taught you manners? You should knock before walking into someone's office. I could've been in an important meeting," he snapped at her. She raised her brows at him, and the smirk on her face wasn't helping his mood. "Where the hell is my secretary, anyway? She should have stopped you."

"You've obviously been terrorizing your office staff, and I told your secretary we were meeting for lunch and that there was no need to buzz you. If you have a problem with that, then you can take it out on me — not her. I think, if you blow up at the poor woman one more time, she's going to walk out the door while she tells you where you can stick your bad attitude," she told him with arrogance.

"So, I guess you're telling me how to run my offices now?" he questioned.

"Obviously someone needs to," she gave right back.

"You drive me to the point of madness," he snapped.

149

"Well, that makes two of us. I don't see why you want to continue this arrangement when we are both so miserable. You're the one who insisted I come down here," she yelled. He knew his staff was getting bits and pieces of their conversation, and he really didn't care.

"I'm hungry. Let's go," he commanded and walked out the door, not trusting himself to touch her. He was in a foul mood, and he'd end up throwing her over his desk. He wanted to bend her to his will but, at the same time, part of his immense attraction for her was due to the fact that she wasn't just another whimpering female, wanting only to please him. He wouldn't mind a little bit of appreciation from her, though.

"Yes, sir," she mumbled. He pretended not to hear her. It was better for both of them that way. As he crossed the offices, he noticed his employees weren't making eye contact with him. He started to feel a bit badly about that. He normally wasn't a bear, and people loved to work for him. He really was going to have to try not to take his frustrations out on his employees. He looked over to his secretary and waited until he got her attention.

"Order lunch for everybody today, and use my credit card. After lunch, those who don't have immediate things to be finished tonight can have the rest of the afternoon off," he said and walked toward the elevators. He smiled as his employees' faces lit up.

"Thank you, Mr. Titan," a few different people called as he entered the elevator. He nodded his head before the doors shut, locking him and Nicole into the small space.

"That was really sweet of you," Nicole told him. Her entire demeanor had relaxed with those few words he'd uttered. He looked at her with surprise. She threw thousand-dollar gifts back in his face with contempt, but he spent a few hundred dollars on lunch for strangers, and she got all warm and fuzzy. He couldn't understand her.

"I'm a nice guy," he said with a leer. He then couldn't take the space between them anymore, so he reached out and pulled her into his arms. She stiffened for about two seconds, and then her body melted into his. Sexual chemistry wasn't something they were lacking. He kissed her with all his pent up anger and need and, by the time the elevator reached the bottom floor, they were both panting.

His security staff acted as if they hadn't seen anything, thankfully. He knew the cameras in the elevators had given them quite a show. If Nicole knew that, she would've been mortified. He was going to speak to his staff and have a panel put in the elevator because he suddenly needed to have a way to turn off those monitors.

He pulled her out into the busy Seattle streets and led her to a small diner. There were so many great little cafés with excellent food in the city, he was constantly being surprised. Nicole thawed out, and they enjoyed a nice lunch together.

When she didn't have herself armed against him, she actually relaxed, and he could see pieces of the teenage girl he'd been in love with so many years before. That had to be the reason he couldn't let her go. He simply had to purge himself of those long ago teenage fantasies. He'd be fine once he'd done that.

"Let's do some shopping," he told her. She wore the same clothing over and over again and-- not that she looked bad in anything she wore — but he was an incredibly wealthy man, and he wouldn't be made a fool.

"I don't want to leave Patsy for too long," she told him, as she followed him from the table to the car waiting for them.

"Patsy has 'round the clock care and will be fine for a few hours," he said with frustration. She looked for any excuse to get away from him, and he wasn't going to allow it.

"I know, but she still needs me," Nicole said. She had to fight her attraction to Ryan every second when she was with him, and it was exhausting. She'd been wobbly ever since their passionate kiss in the elevator. That may be something he did on a daily basis, but it knocked her off her feet, and it took every ounce of her concentration to keep up in conversation with him.

She also found it extremely difficult to keep maintaining her distance from the man when he was charming, such as when he was buying his staff lunch. He hadn't actually admitted to being a bear around them, but he'd apologized, nonetheless, with his gesture. She was sure he was already forgiven by his staff. The man had a charismatic way about him that simply made people want to jump to please him.

They arrived at some top end mall she'd never been to. The cheapest store in the place was way beyond what her budget would allow. She was a bit self-conscious, walking into the building in her current jeans and t-shirt combo. She held her head up high, though, because clothes didn't make the person. She didn't need fancy items to wear to make her as good as the other women around her.

As they walked around, she couldn't help but notice the snobby looks she received from some women and the looks of envy from others. Most of the women probably thought she was a poor relative of Ryan's because he certainly fit in with the crowd in his custom made Armani suit and Italian loafers.

They walked into a store, and the clerk approached them eagerly, practically purring at Ryan. Nicole felt a slight pang of jealousy and had to fight it down. Ryan grinned down at her — far too brilliantly, in Nicole's opinion.

"How can I help you?" she asked Ryan, completely ignoring Nicole, who was a bit irritated by that.

"We need to purchase an entire wardrobe. I'm sure you'll be able to help us," he practically purred back at her. The woman actually blushed a bit at his brilliant smile, and Nicole had to suck in the words she wanted to shout at the piranha.

Then she realized they were in a woman's shop and what he was intending. Her face turned scarlet as the woman turned toward her for an assessment. Nicole could see the woman wanted to know who she was, and she could also see the woman was hoping she was his little sister.

"I can certainly help you with new clothing. Please follow me," she said and sauntered off, moving her hips much more than needed.

"What do you think you're doing?" Nicole accused underneath her breath, certainly not wanting the very elegant woman to overhear her.

"I'm purchasing you some clothes," he said. He then looked at her as if she wasn't too bright, since they were standing in a store.

"I didn't ask for you to purchase me clothing, nor do I want new clothes," she hissed at him and started to walk out the door. She almost got out the door, but at the last second, Ryan snaked his arm out and grabbed her.

"You'll allow me to do this. You need to dress a certain way for occasions I want you to attend," he said. They glared at each other for several moments. Nicole was trying to figure out how to get out of the store without making a scene.

"Are you coming?" the saleslady asked from the back of the store, some concern in her voice. She was most likely worried about losing the huge commission he'd promised her.

"Yes, we are," Ryan said and literally dragged Nicole to the back of the store. Before she knew it, the lovely woman had her stripped of her clothing, and Nicole was left standing in nothing but her bra and panties, while the woman took her measurements.

Ryan sat there, cool as ice, as he watched her. Nicole turned her face away and had to fight back tears, she was so angry. The saleswoman, whose name was Barbie — *Very fitting*, Nicole thought snidely — brought different items out for Ryan's approval.

Nicole refused to comment on a single item, so Ryan picked everything. She didn't need to try anything on, as the clothes were chosen from the measurements the woman had taken earlier. The entire ordeal lasted a few hours and, by the time they were done, Nicole had a raging headache and couldn't have described a single item Ryan chose. He had all the clothes boxed. Then he had his driver come and haul them all out to his vehicle.

Nicole figured he'd just wasted an incredible amount of money because she wouldn't wear one thing he'd picked. Ryan could save them for his next mistress. She wouldn't be bought.

They reached the office, and she gladly left his car and headed over toward her own. She was done talking to him and wanted to go back to the house, have a hot bath, and forget the day had happened. If she stayed around him too much longer, she'd end up smacking him in his gorgeous face.

CHAPTER SEVEN

Ryan had the opportunity to work on an amazing historical site in Italy. It was the first time in his life he wanted to turn any project away. In the end, it was simply too great of an opportunity to let it go. He couldn't believe he was even considering not doing it, but Patsy wasn't ready to leave the country, and there was no way he could take Nicole. She'd be miserable wondering how her sister was.

A month quickly passed with good and bad results. Nicole still fought him every step of the way, and his hunger for her was as strong as it had been from the first day, but he still woke to find her gone. She didn't try climbing into another bed, but he'd find her on the sofa, watching a movie, or out in the garden. He couldn't complain and keep her locked to his bed twenty-four-seven, but he'd like to.

Ryan decided to force himself to go on the trip. He refused to let her alter his lifestyle, especially since she wasn't giving him anything of herself emotionally. But, even beyond that, the trip would be good. Maybe when he was gone she'd miss him and start appreciating the things he did for her. He was happy and hopeful about her possibly missing him. He was also afraid he was going to be the one aching and miserable.

He could swear she was a witch and had him under some kind of a spell. She even got along spectacularly with all of his family members. He seemed to be the only one who ever got under her skin. He hadn't once in his adult life lasted so long with any woman. He couldn't seem to get enough

160

of her, even when she was snapping at him. It figured he wanted more than anything the one thing he should cut ties with.

"Hey, where did you go?" Derek asked.

"Sorry, my mind drifted off," Ryan told his cousin.

"Yeah, I remember those days. I bet your thoughts were filled with a dark-haired beauty," Derek said with a waggle of his brows.

"No, of course not. I'm thinking about my upcoming trip," Ryan lied smoothly.

"When are you leaving?"

"I have to take off tonight. I won't be back for at least a month--maybe longer. Hopefully, by then, I'll have some more control over myself," Ryan told him. Derek actually had the gall to laugh, which caused Ryan to glare. That only made Derek laugh even harder. He guessed he deserved it, as he'd pushed Derek's buttons when he'd been miserable.

"I have a trip next week in that direction, so I'll stop by and see what you're working on. I haven't been able to take Jasmine out in a while, and I think she'd really love Rome," Derek told him with a sappy look in his eye.

"Seriously, Derek. You're disgustingly pleasant now. What the hell happened to the corporate powerhouse?"

"Jasmine happened. I didn't know I could be so happy, but man, if I'm away from her for even a night, I feel empty," Derek said. Ryan's gut clenched at those words. He was forcing himself to be away from Nicole for much longer than one night. He wasn't his cousin, though, and he wouldn't allow himself to think about it. It was a good thought, at least.

"I feel like a freaking third wheel around you and Drew now," Ryan said, feeling a little bit sorry for himself. He loved his cousins' spouses, but both of them were over the moon with happiness. He felt like they were sharing some great secret he couldn't possibly understand.

"I'll see if Drew and Trinity want to join me on the trip. I don't think Trinity's ever been to Rome either. I don't know if I can drag them away from the kids, though."

"Yeah, yeah. You guys can all come and throw your happiness in my face," Ryan grumbled. He may have been complaining, but he'd be happy to have his family come and see one of his projects.

"All joking aside, I think you have something special with Nicole. Take my advice and let down your defenses, and maybe you'll get that same sappy look on your face," Derek told him.

"I'll pass on that."

"Yeah, that's what I said too. Let's see if you last as long as I did," Derek said, with a knowing look on his face. Derek took off, and Ryan tried to put Nicole out of his mind while he started focusing on his project. He really did enjoy Rome. It was a beautiful place, and the project he was taking on was the biggest and oldest he'd worked on yet. It would consume him wholeheartedly, which was a good thing.

###

Ryan slammed the hammer down with far more force than was needed. He'd been on the job for over a month, and sitting at a desk, behind the scenes, wasn't even enough to quell his bad mood. He couldn't believe he was still unable to get Nicole out of his mind. He'd even called her several times, making up excuses, but the real reason was just to hear her voice. He was going home that day. He couldn't take being apart from her any longer. He still reassured himself he simply needed to get her out of his system.

His family had shown up and been suitably impressed with his project, but even the normal joy he felt in restoring a historic site was gone. He'd taken a few days off to tour the city with his family, but his smile had been fake, and his joy had been subdued. He continued to hammer away his frustration, and when he bent yet another nail, he decided to call it a day.

He was ready to head home and take back what was his. He couldn't get her off his mind, so the next best thing was to go home and see where things were going to lead. He had a real problem, though, because he'd gotten really attached to

Patsy. Hell, she was still a kid, even if she was a teenager.

The first time she said "I love you" to him, so casually, his heart had jumped into his throat. There was no way he wanted to kick her out of his home. She seemed to be doing so well, and her grades were thriving. He refused to think about any of that right then. His only thought was getting home and taking Nicole to his bed, where she belonged.

Nicole stretched as the sunlight filtered through the window, waking her up. She'd been living at Ryan's for three months, and she'd fallen in love with the place. He'd been gone over the past month, and she'd never admit it, but she missed him like crazy. He'd called her a few times, and she got off the phone aching to be held by him again. She was angry with herself for being so weak.

Her room was a dream and larger than her old apartment. She lay there, enjoying the softness of the mattress, and yet being in it alone filled her with a sense of emptiness. She couldn't believe how attached she'd gotten to Ryan again in such a short amount of time. She figured she'd never really stopped loving him in the first place, and being around him again was like a knife through her heart.

Nicole jumped from her bed, quickly showered, got dressed and headed outside. She spent every moment she could outside when the weather allowed. The morning was starting off beautiful and warm, which was highly unusual for Seattle, home of the rain.

She took off down one of the trails on a jog, enjoying the little bit of heaven not far outside of the city limits. When she jogged along the trail, she felt like she was in a park instead of a yard. She ran out of steam quickly, which was normal lately, and she didn't understand it. She was used to going and going day in and out and didn't know why her energy levels had been so depleted lately.

As Nicole walked along, she thought about her baby sister. She loved how well Patsy was doing. She was back in school and healthier than ever before. She'd fallen in love at the better high school, which Derek had insisted she attend. She had new friends who'd been at the house a lot, and she was even getting ready for her first dance.

Nicole had felt guilty about spending more of Ryan's money, but when he'd found out about the dance, he'd insisted she buy Patsy the best dress out there. Jasmine and Trinity were far more knowing about the latest fashions than Nicole was, so she'd asked them to come along with them, and the sisters-in-law had enthusiastically agreed.

Pasty had the best day ever, as the girls not only picked out a dress but new shoes and accessories, and even a small tiara to wear. The girls had then dragged them both from shop to shop, where Patsy had been loaded down with an entire new wardrobe. The girls had snuck several items in there for Nicole as well, and she was cringing to think what the final bill had tallied out to.

She hadn't had the heart to say no to Patsy, though, as she hadn't seen her little sister's eyes light up with pleasure that intense ever. The day hadn't been completed until they all went in for pedicures and manicures. Patsy had even gotten fake nails put on for her dance. She'd been prancing around the house ever since.

That night when Ryan called, Patsy jumped on the phone and talked for about fifteen minutes. She went through her entire day and all the amazing clothes she'd gotten. She didn't have any clue he was the one footing the bill. As she got ready to hand the phone over to Nicole, she told him she loved him, as only a teenager could, and Nicole had to fight back the tears.

She knew she'd be considered a horrible person if she ever tried to take Patsy away from the home where she'd made new friends. But wouldn't she have to leave eventually--when Patsy was done with school, if not sooner? Whenever Ryan was sick of her, they were out. She had a feeling he'd allow Patsy to stay, though, as he seemed attached to her.

Nicole felt a stinging in her leg, which snapped her back to the present, and she looked down to see red running downward. She panicked for a moment, thinking something had bitten her and she was pouring blood, but as she looked closer, she realized it was paint. She smiled, as she realized the kids were out having a paintball gun fight again. She'd run into them several times.

"Hey, I'm an innocent bystander," she called out good-naturedly.

"Nicole? Sorry. We didn't know you were out here," the oldest boy, Jacob, said as he came running up, looking very guilty. He had several friends trailing behind him, all with the same expressions of guilt on their faces. "I heard a noise over here and thought it was one of the guys," he said, as a slight blush stole over his cheeks.

"I'm fine, Jacob. It looks like you guys are having a great time," she reassured him.

"We are. Do you want to join us?" he offered. The other boys nodded their heads encouragingly.

"No, I have to get back, but maybe some other time," she told them. She turned around to walk back toward the house, and the boys all ran off in the other direction, shouting and firing at the same time. She smiled to herself. Jacob was Ryan's nephew--well, technically his cousin, but the three men were more brothers than cousins, and the kids called both their fathers' cousins "Uncle." She was impressed with the very tightly knit family.

Nicole finally reached the house and realized the paintball hit her harder than she originally thought. She had a slight limp and a huge knot on her leg. She stepped into the kitchen so she could clean up when a shadow nearly scared her to death.

"What happened to your leg?" Ryan asked. She was speechless for a moment, as she looked up and saw him standing before her. She hadn't expected him back for a few more weeks, and she was worried by how much she wanted to throw her arms around the man who haunted her dreams each night.

"I got shot with a paintball, but it looks far worse than it is. This is only paint," she said and bent to run her finger over the paint.

Ryan sucked in the breath he'd been holding. He'd missed her so much, and when he'd arrived home and had not been able to find her, he'd gone a bit crazy. He'd thought she might have left him, but her clothes were there, and Patsy's room was filled with her possessions. He smiled to think how well Patsy had settled in. At least one of them had no problem with him spoiling them. Nicole acted like he was committing a sin when he tried to give her anything. It was downright insulting.

He had more money than he could possibly ever spend, but Nicole didn't want to allow him to buy her a simple pair of jeans. He wouldn't allow people to think he mistreated her in any way. He'd purchase her things, even if he had to literally take her into the dressing room and dress her himself. He got hard just thinking about that scenario.

He stared at her--from her toes to the top of her head. She was make-up free with her hair thrown back in a sloppy ponytail, and she was wearing loose workout clothes. She'd never looked sexier. Damn, he was in a really bad state.

"How did you get shot?"

"Oh, your nephews were having a paintball war, and I was in the wrong place at the wrong time. It could've been worse. They might've been going for the kill shot," she said with a laugh.

His lips rose slightly at the corners. "I missed you," he said before he could stop himself. He hadn't meant for it to slip out, but from the gleam in her eyes, it had been the right thing to say. He had a feeling she'd missed him too, although he didn't think he could get her to admit it.

"Um . . . I . . . um . . . need to . . . um . . . go get this off of me," she stuttered, sounding more like a middle school child than a full-grown adult. Nicole quickly fled the room and never saw the smile split across Ryan's face. It was the first genuine smile he felt cross his features since the night he dragged her from that restaurant.

He began whistling as he followed her up the stairs. He'd wait for her to get out of the shower and then give them what they both so desperately wanted. His aroused body was making it difficult to climb the stairs, but the pain was worth it. Soon she'd be relieving that for him.

CHAPTER EIGHT

"Where the hell have you been?" Ryan asked furiously as Nicole walked in the door. He'd apparently come home early from work, and she hadn't been here. She knew he didn't like not knowing where she was.

"Not that it's any of your business, but I was at work," she snapped back at him. He'd been back for a week, and though they made love nightly, their days were not so pleasant. He was still highly demanding, and she was still trying to assert her own independence.

She had zero doubt she was in love with the man, but she also knew she was simply a plaything for him, and he'd eventually grow bored with her. Then she'd be devastated all over again. To top all that, she had a bad feeling she was pregnant. She'd been ignoring it for months, but her stomach was starting to thicken, and she'd been so exhausted.

She could pass off the thickening stomach to the amount of food she had consumed, but the unusual desire for foods she'd never liked before, the complete exhaustion, and the mood swings were a dead giveaway. She'd refused to take a test. Then she'd know for sure, and she'd have to break the news to Ryan. She wasn't ready for that.

###

"Everything you do is my business. How quickly you forget what we agreed upon," he snapped. He was beyond mad that she'd taken one of her worthless jobs again when he was willing to provide everything she and Patsy needed. She allowed him to spoil Patsy, but she refused to wear the jewelry he bought her, and she wore the same old clothes she'd come to his home with over and over again. It was really making him angry.

Every other woman he'd ever dated had tried to get every last thing they could out of him. Now he finally had a woman he wanted to buy things for, and she tossed them back in his face. He'd already had a frustrating day at the office, which was why he'd come home early in the first place, and she was now aggravating his mood even further. He'd hoped being with her would calm him down. It wasn't happening.

"You'll quit whatever crappy job you took because I want you home when I need you," he told her. She looked at him like he was insane for a moment. He could see she was trying to decide whether to yell at him or walk away. Finally, she started laughing. He stood there in complete shock. No one ever laughed at him. He didn't like it.

"I won't quit my job. I happen to have found one that I love. I know my measly little paycheck for two weeks doesn't even compare to what you make in one hour, but it's my money, and I'm earning it on my own. I've told you before I'll pay back every penny you've spent on Patsy and me. I need a job to be able to afford to do that."

"I've told you I don't want a dime from you," he said for the hundredth time.

"Well, I don't take handouts, and I'll be paying you."

"Why the hell do you have to be so stubborn all the time? It's ridiculous. You're doing nothing but hurting yourself and your sister. Grow up, and stop acting like a damn child," he said through clenched teeth.

"Just because you have far more money than any one person should ever have doesn't mean you can throw it in my face. If I want to pay you back then I'll do it, whether I have to stuff it down your throat or not," she told him stubbornly.

"I can't even talk to you," he shouted as he ran his fingers through his hair once again.

"Well, that goes both ways, you arrogant jerk."

"I guess, then, I'll have to drag you away from this job you have. I've done it once. Don't think I won't do it again," he threatened.

"I don't think you're going to be able to do that," she smirked at him, which caused his blood to boil even more.

"I can figure out easily where you're working, Nicole, so don't act so cocky."

"Oh, I don't have a problem telling you where I work. My co-workers will rip you apart if you so much as lay one finger on me while I'm there," she said far too smugly.

Images of her working at a strip club with bouncers went through his mind. He could think of no other place where she'd foolishly believe he wouldn't try and drag her out. He'd certainly drag her out of a strip club and would look forward to the fight.

"If you're working at some trashy night club or bar, I swear I'll go to jail for pounding the crap out of whoever has dared to come near you there," he yelled.

A shocked look crossed Nicole's face, and he saw her shiver.Ryan felt immediate relief. Thank goodness she hadn't been that stupid.

"If you must know, I'm working with Jasmine and Trinity at their place," she said smugly.Ryan blew out his breath as he realized she was right. There was no way in hell he'd try and drag her out of there. Jasmine and Trinity would tear him apart. There wasn't a man on the planet he feared, but his cousins' wives were a whole different matter.

She once again laughed at him, obviously loving that she'd won the argument. She took off up the stairs like she didn't have a care in the world.

He stared in shock. She laughed in his face and then outright defied him. To top off everything, she had the gall to walk away when he wasn't finished with their argument. Ryan knew, logically, he should let her go so he could calm himself down, but he had never been one to walk away from a fight.

He slowly stalked her up the stairs and found her in their bedroom. His temper was already escalated and, seeing her in their room, in those same raggedy clothes made him snap. He was sick and tired of seeing her lessen herself by wearing rags.

Nicole turned around, and the look on Ryan's face terrified her. She didn't think she'd ever seen him so furious. Maybe she'd pushed it a little bit far. She was thinking it might be much wiser to apologize and tuck tail and run. She wasn't going to quit her job, though. She was getting ready to say she was sorry when he opened his mouth and infuriated her all over again.

"I've bought you new clothes, and you still choose to wear those rags. I demand you toss them out now," he yelled at her.

Her hackles were immediately up again. "I'd rather be naked than to wear your charity handouts," she shouted right back. Her eyes widened at the look that came into his eyes.

Ryan walked into her closet and ripped her precious few items off the hangers. Then he walked over to her dresser and took out the few pairs of her underclothing she'd brought with her. He tossed it all on the bed and stalked towards her.

She backed up, like anyone would do when being approached by a predator. Nicole was terrified and yet incredibly aroused at the same time. He was so masculine, and she couldn't tear her gaze away from him.

"Take them off," he said in a deadly calm voice.

"Not on your life," she spat back, but her words were belied by the breathless quality in her voice. He walked up to her and yanked the shirt off. Then he tossed her on the bed, causing her to gasp. He pulled her jeans off next, leaving her in nothing but her bra and panties. She was incredibly grateful she was wearing one of the pairs the girls had made her get, or she was sure he would've ripped those off as well.

Nicole was breathing heavily as his eyes raked over her exposed skin. Catching her by surprise, he stooped down and grabbed the clothes he'd taken off her, and then walked out of the room. It took her a few moments before the shock wore off, and then she went in search of something with which to cover herself. She couldn't go chasing him through the house in nothing but her underclothes.

By the time she got a robe on and followed him down the stairs, she couldn't find him anywhere. Suddenly, a smell hit her, and she gasped again. *He wouldn't dare*, she thought, as she made a dash toward the backyard. Her eyes widened in shock and fury as she saw what he was doing. She came running out the door, and he turned and gave her a victorious smile.

He was standing in front of the huge fire pit they used for bonfires, and her clothes were going up in flames. She couldn't believe he'd burn her clothes. He must've doused them in gasoline first because the flames were huge. There was no chance she could salvage them.

"How dare you burn my clothes," she yelled, seeing red. He winked at her, and she wanted to claw his eyes out. She was so mad, she was beyond reasonable thinking. The staff had seen what was going on and had all scurried away, no one brave enough to come between the two of them in the middle of a fight.

"I do whatever I want to," he said in a mocking voice.

"Well, you know what? Let's just add more fuel to the fire," she shouted. She ripped off her robe and tossed it into the flames. She then pulled her bra off and tossed it in. She was so mad she didn't even think about the fact she was stripping in the middle of the day, where anyone could possibly walk by.

###

Ryan watched her strip the robe, exposing her luscious breasts to him before his brain kicked in again. Anyone could walk out the back door and see her standing there nearly naked. She may have been trying to prove a point, but all she'd done was turn his anger into complete and total desire.

He grabbed her in his arms before she could strip the panties off and then, shielding her body with his own, carried her into the house and took the back stairs to their bedroom. She yelled and pounded on him with her fists the entire way, which only fueled his desire. He'd tame her in the best way he could possibly imagine.

He unceremoniously tossed her onto their bed, and she was so stunned it gave him a few precious seconds to strip himself. When she realized what he was doing, she quickly tried to scramble off the bed, but he grabbed her and pinned her beneath him. Her hands were locked above her head, and he was fully pressed into her nearly naked body. The only thing stopping him from sinking deep inside her heat was a tiny scrap of silk.

He was so throbbing hard, he was sure he could rip through the tiny piece of material. They glared at one another, locked there on the bed. She squirmed underneath him, which only caused his erection to jump with painful intensity.

"Don't you dare touch me, you arrogant pig," she said through clenched teeth. He would've come to his senses and let her go if he would've seen fear in her eyes--or even pure fury. But he saw desire quickly consuming her, and it showed in her very readable face. He could feel her nipples, which were obviously peaked into hard nubs, pressing against his chest. They both had a light sheen of sweat breaking out on their bodies, and neither of them was breathing normally.

"Don't touch you like this?" he questioned as he moved his mouth down her neck, where he gently bit on the sensitive skin where her shoulder met her smooth throat. He licked the spot and ran open-mouthed kisses along her neck and up her throat. He licked the edge of her lips but didn't kiss her quite yet.

"Or like this?" he said huskily as he ground his hips into the heat between her thighs. She was shaking beneath him, and he could see she was trying to fight herself far harder than she was trying to fight him.

"Or this?" he growled before he finally connected their mouths and slipped his tongue inside. He still had her hands pinned above her head, and her squirming began in earnest but for an entirely different reason than before.

Her anger had fled, and now he could see she was writhing underneath him in pleasure. He released her hands, and she moved them into his hair to pull him closer. He ripped the sides of her panties and, not being able to wait a single second longer, he thrust inside her heat. She was wet and tight, showing him she was as turned on as he was.

She may hate him at the moment, but she wanted him with as much passion as he wanted her. He grabbed her hips in his hands, so he could angle her heat up higher. He wanted to be sunk so deeply inside her, he wouldn't know where he ended and she began. She was crying out in pleasure as he pounded in and out of her.

"Say you want me," he growled at her. She shook her head *no*. Even in the throes of passion, she didn't want to surrender to him. He needed her surrender, and as much as it caused him actual physical pain, he buried himself deeply in her and stopped moving. She squirmed underneath him, so close to her peak, needing him to move. "Say it," he again demanded through clenched teeth. She glared at him through her desire-filled eyes, almost sobbing with her frustration and need for him to move within her.

"I want you," she finally cried out. He rewarded them both by thrusting in and out of her with so much frantic speed they both tumbled over the edge within seconds. She squeezed his erection with her intense orgasm and cried out as he spilled inside of her. It was the longest and most intense pleasure he'd ever felt in his life.

After the shaking in both of their bodies stopped, he collapsed against her, not having the strength to move one muscle in his body. He was trying to simply get his breathing back under control. No woman had ever had the power to make him snap that much. He noticed she was squirming beneath him and realized he was most likely crushing her under his weight. Hell, he weighed more than twice as much as she did. He turned their bodies, refusing to let her go.

He could tell she didn't have the energy to fight him anymore, not after the intense pleasure she'd just received. Nicole allowed him to keep her tucked at his side. They both fell asleep from the strenuous fight and love-making. Ryan realized he was glad it happened. He may have burned her clothing in anger, but at least they were gone and the lovemaking alone had been worth it. He fell asleep with a smile on his face.

###

Nicole woke up wrapped around Ryan's body. She felt her face heat up with embarrassment. She couldn't believe the fight they'd had. She also couldn't believe how much she'd needed him after it was all over. She'd felt like she'd explode if he didn't relieve the ache in her body.

She shifted slightly and tried to untangle herself from him. She wanted to run away and hide for a while. After they'd both passed out, she'd awoken again, only to be ravished by him with even more intensity than before. She knew it must be the middle of the night, but she was wide awake and she had to get out of there.

"Don't even think about it," she heard Ryan say, and his grip tightened on her body.

She tensed. "I need to use the restroom," she said in excuse. She couldn't see his face, and she was glad he couldn't see hers because she knew it was flaming scarlet in embarrassment.

"I'll come and hunt you down if you aren't back in less than five minutes," he warned her before finally releasing her from his arms. Nicole quickly ran to the bathroom, where she washed her face and stared at herself in the mirror.

She ignored his threat and jumped into the shower. The hot water cascading over her sore muscles caused a groan to escape her lips. The water felt wonderful. She knew Ryan was going to be irritated, but she didn't care about anything at that moment except for the water running down her skin.

Ryan heard the shower start and sat up with irritation. The insufferable woman had to defy him no matter what he said. He figured, after yesterday, she'd take him a bit more seriously. He looked at the clock and saw it was two in the morning.

His stomach growled, reminding him they'd both missed dinner. He threw a robe on and ran down to the kitchen, loaded up a tray with food, and dashed back to their room. He was relieved when he heard the shower still running. He was beginning to enjoy chasing his woman.

He set the tray on the bed, stripped the robe off, and headed into the bathroom to join her in the shower. He could feed both of his hungers in a few minutes' time.

###

Nicole gasped when Ryan's arms came around her in the shower. She shouldn't have been surprised he'd follow her in, but she'd been just about finished and figured he'd fallen back asleep.

Ryan said nothing as he took her in his arms and reminded her she was his. The things he did to her made it almost worth being under his power.

They climbed from the shower together, and he wrapped her in a huge fluffy towel. She enjoyed his towels and didn't think she'd ever be able to go back to the scratchy kind, which had never bothered her before.

When she stepped into the room, she was embarrassed by the loud growling in her stomach the smell of the food caused. Ryan raised his brow at her and gave her a smile. She chose to ignore him and made a dash for the food. She didn't care how it made her look.

"When will you actually start listening to me?" Ryan asked her in such a conversational tone of voice it took a few moments for the words to actually sink in.

"I'm not your possession, your call girl, or your employee, and therefore I don't have to listen to you," she stated back in the same conversational tone.

"You'll learn."

"I wouldn't hold your breath in anticipation of that. No, wait a minute. Go ahead and do just that. I'm sure it won't take too long," she said in a sugary sweet voice and batted her eyes at him.

Ryan laughed out loud. He really could get used to her being a part of his life on a permanent basis. She was good for his huge ego, or at least for taking it down a notch or two. He didn't think he'd ever get her tamed, but he was sure going to enjoy trying.

They finished up the food, and Ryan shut the light off and pulled her down next to him. Unbelievably, he was still tired. He never slept more than about six hours a night, but he had a feeling, by the time they got up, it would be more likely ten hours that particular night.

Nicole was stiff in his arms, stubborn as always. Apparently that got too uncomfortable for her, though. After a while, she finally relaxed, and they both fell asleep.

Ryan knew they'd both won some of the smaller battles that evening, but overall he'd won the war. He'd gotten exactly what he wanted, with her in his bed. He'd make sure he woke up with her still in his arms. It may have been a small thing, but to him it was a matter of a line being drawn in the sand and her learning not to cross it.

CHAPTER NINE

"There's absolutely no way I'm going to another one of those parties with you, and that's final," Nicole said. She placed her arms across her chest and glared at Ryan.

"We have an agreement, and if I want to parade you around to ten of those parties a week, you won't only go, but you'll do it with a smile plastered across your face," he yelled at her.

He hadn't yet seen her put her foot down. He may have thought she'd been stubborn before, but the last party he'd made her attend had been miserable, and the women had been piranhas. Neither Jasmine nor Trinity had been there, and she'd fought tears the entire time. She wouldn't put herself through that again.

"I don't care about the stupid agreement. You're expecting too much," she told him.

"The only reason you were miserable at the last party was because of your own stupid stubbornness," he mocked her. She'd refused to wear the dress he'd purchased or the jewelry that lined her drawer. Instead, she'd worn her own sale rack dress which, Ryan had told her, made her look like she should be attending a backyard barbecue. Of course, the socialites had also ripped her to shreds.

Nicole knew he was angry with her for refusing his gifts, and he ignored her most of the night. They'd both walked away from the evening ticked off. He didn't even want to go to the stupid party they were fighting about. He'd only accepted the invitation because he wanted to punish her, which made her just as angry at him as he was at her.

"Well you can take your party and stick it up your . . ."

He didn't let her finish her words. He grabbed her in his arms and smashed his mouth down on hers.

"You'll be ready by seven tonight," he told her and walked from the room. She smiled at the closed door. He really had another thing coming if he thought he'd get his way. If he didn't like how she was behaving, then he could kick her out. She didn't like the feeling that thought caused in her gut. She may think he was a pompous jerk half the time, but he was also the boy she'd loved more than any other.

What really scared her was that she was falling for the man he now was. He was beautiful, caring, family-oriented, and made love with so much passion she never wanted to let him go afterward.

Nicole got ready for work and left her room. She crept down the stairs, grateful Ryan was nowhere around. She jumped into her car with a smile. Her car was another point of contention between them. He'd actually had the gall to go out and buy her a new car. It sat untouched in his oversized garage. She refused to drive it. She wanted to, more than she'd ever let him know, but she was afraid she'd like it more than she should.

It was a beautiful red convertible with all the bells and whistles, and if he'd been in love with her, she would've been more than happy to accept the generous gift, but that wasn't the case. It was a gift for a mistress, and she couldn't accept it without feeling horrible about herself. Because of this, she wouldn't accept anything he tried to buy for her. If she caved in, even once, she'd lose a piece of herself, and she couldn't let that happen.

He was already getting her in his bed every night, and she loved each minute, though she wouldn't admit it to him. She was beginning to want what she could never have. She turned the key in the ignition and smiled victoriously when the motor turned over and started.

"That's a real good girl," she praised her car. It drove her sister nuts when she talked to the car like it was a human being, but she didn't care. She figured her words of praise were the only things keeping her car going.

She drove to work--only a few miles away, thankfully — and felt her tension evaporate. She loved working with Jasmine and Trinity at their shop. It was an amazing place with a café, floral department and unique gifts. She couldn't imagine how satisfying it must be for them to know it was theirs and no one could take it away.

She knew their husbands had more money than they would ever spend, and they didn't need to work, but they, like her, needed something of their own.

"Good morning, Nicole. How are you today?" Trinity said as she walked in the door.

"I'm great. How about you?"

"Wonderful. Now, come sit with us and have some breakfast. Jasmine just made the most incredible pastries I've ever eaten in my life," Trinity demanded. Nicole felt a bit guilty sitting on the job. She didn't want to take advantage of her friends.

"I really should get to work," she told them.

"Nonsense. As you can see, we don't have any customers right now, and the whole idea of having a place like this is so we can have our own place to gossip and get away from the house," Jasmine said. She set an overflowing plate of pastries on the table with a pot of specially made coffee. The delicious aroma filled every breathable space in the store. Nicole was sure she was going to gain a hundred pounds while working with these girls. She'd never before had a job where she had so much down time.

"I think my clothes are fitting tighter just being in here," she said with a laugh. The women chatted for a while, enjoying each other's company. A couple of the other employees came in and moved around the shop, but it was a really casual atmosphere.

"So, if you could do anything, what would it be?" Trinity asked her. Nicole missed the sly look between the two women.

"I'd love to have some place like this, actually. This is amazing. I'd enjoy having my own scrapbooking store someday. I haven't had time to create any albums of my own in years. The cost to get set up is expensive, and with as much as I've always worked, I couldn't justify spending the money," she said with a sigh.

"Oh my gosh. It's so interesting you mention that because Jasmine and I have talked about expanding and bringing in more products," Trinity said with a smile.

"That would be so great if you brought in scrapbooking supplies. I know you wouldn't regret it. It's such a popular craft. I know you don't need money, but it's a huge earning potential. I'd love to help you pick out some products, and I could even teach some of the classes," Nicole said with real enthusiasm.

"How about if you're running your own scrapbooking store?" Jasmine asked. Nicole was filled with a desire she didn't even want to think about. There was no way she could take on her own business. She'd never be able to get the loans and, if it failed, as so many small businesses did, she wouldn't be able to recover. She already owed Ryan her left arm and leg. She couldn't pay for a business and pay him back too.

"That would be such a dream, but now isn't the right time in my life to go into such a huge investment," Nicole told them sadly.

"Well, you have two new best friends who already own the space. It wouldn't take Ryan long to build an addition, and you have nothing to lose, as we're already established. We're going to invest in you because we know, beyond a shadow of a doubt, you'll excel at it," Trinity told her. Nicole's eyes filled with tears at the confidence her friends had in her. It was such an overwhelming feeling. It left her speechless.

She finally got up and gave them each a huge hug. She couldn't keep the tear from sliding down her face at having met two women who were so caring and wonderful. She really wished she'd known Jasmine more during their school years because she had the feeling they would've been inseparable.

"I appreciate it. I really do, and maybe later I can think about doing that. Not right now. For now, I'll help the two of you because I love working here," Nicole told them. "Now, I have to use the restroom," she added and made her escape before she burst into tears.

Jasmine and Trinity waited until she was out of earshot to make plans. They knew she wanted it. She was just scared. They were determined to give her something she could be proud of. Jasmine called Ryan and told him they wanted him to build on an addition. They didn't tell him what it was for, either. They couldn't risk any chance of Nicole finding out about it until the moment it was ready.

They would certainly be keeping her busy over the next month with purchasing all the supplies to fill the new addition. The girls could hardly wait.

###

Nicole finished her day and headed out of the shop. Trinity and Jasmine had left earlier, and she'd drug her feet, not wanting to get back to the house early and fight with Ryan.

She jumped into her car, and it started once again, making her incredibly happy. It was just starting to get dark out, and she was feeling really tired. She wanted a hot bath and her soft bed. She got a few miles down the road, and her car spluttered and died. She coasted it to the side of the road and tried to get it going for about fifteen minutes. She finally gave up and settled for walking. The place was only about a couple more miles, but it might as well have been twenty with the exhaustion she felt.

She was creeped out by the dark and had to take a few deep breaths to work up the courage for her trek. She got out of the car and started walking along the side of the road. A few cars passed by her, but she kept her head down, and they kept going. She'd never get in the car with a stranger, no matter how harmless they looked or how great the neighborhood seemed.

###

Ryan paced by the door, waiting for her to come in. When she was still not there by six, he called the shop. There was no answer, and he knew she must have left at least an hour earlier. He was beyond angry she'd gone somewhere else. He grabbed his keys and decided to go searching for her. Of course, she refused to take the cell phone he'd gotten her. She refused to use anything he got her. She only wore the bare minimum of clothes he'd purchased because he'd burned all her original clothes. He didn't regret doing that, especially considering how the night had ended.

He drove down the route he knew she'd take home and passed right by her, walking on the side of the road, because he hadn't expected her to be there. When he reached her car, he started to panic a bit. He jumped out of his car and walked over to the piece of junk. He knew it was going to eventually leave her stranded. It was infuriating she wouldn't use the perfectly good car he'd bought her. Well, her rusted car was heading to the junkyard, and there was nothing else she could do but drive the car he'd bought.

He drove back the way he'd come, much slower, praying he'd spot her and that nothing bad had happened. He saw her about a mile from her car and breathed a sigh of relief. He pulled up next to her and opened his door.

"Get in, Nicole," he told her through clenched teeth. She should never have been in that death trap in the first place, and seeing her walking along the dark road pushed his short temper over the edge of reason.

Nicole took one look at Ryan's face and decided there was no way she was getting in his car. She was still mad at him about their earlier fight, and his tone set her own temper to the boiling point.

"No thank you," she said and picked up her pace. Ryan was so stunned by her refusal, she got a few yards ahead of him before he snapped out of it and gunned the engine. He pulled in front of her and leapt from the car.

He said nothing else, as he didn't trust his voice. He simply picked her up and threw her over his shoulder. Nicole immediately started pounding on his back and demanded he put her down. They were both breathing heavily by the time he dumped her into his passenger seat. She tried to get back out of the car, and he saw red.

"I swear to you, Nicole, if you get out of this car, I'll tie you down in the trunk," he threatened her. He leaned over her, his face only inches from her own. He could tell by the look on her face that she knew he meant what he said. She didn't test him. She sat back, her arms across her chest, and stared out the window, refusing to speak to him.

Ryan drove increasingly fast toward home. He wanted to throttle her, so he knew it wasn't a good idea for them to remain alone. He knew he'd never physically abuse her, but he still might say something he'd regret at a later time.

They arrived at the house. He got out of the car and came around her side before she even had the chance to unbuckle her seat belt. She glared as he reached over and unsnapped it. Then he took her arm and led her inside.

She tried to pull away from him, but he wasn't letting that happen. He pulled her after him, straight into the den. He pushed her onto the couch and glared, letting her know she needed to stay exactly where she was. He walked to the liquor cabinet, poured himself a generous amount of bourbon, and gulped it down. The burning feeling, as it washed down his throat, eased his temper. He took a deep breath and headed to the phone.

Nicole watched him wearily as he picked it up. He spoke for a few minutes before she realized what he was doing. He'd called a wrecking yard and ordered her car to be destroyed. She came unglued.

"How dare you have my car destroyed? You call them back right now and tell them I want it to go to the shop," she demanded of him.

"There's no chance in hell you're driving that car again. Do you know what could've happened to you out there on that dark road? You're incredibly lucky it was me who found you and not some sick and demented fool," he yelled right back.

"I don't call it lucky, you being the one to come to my rescue. I would've rather taken my chances with a psycho," she said, too angry to even think about what she was saying. He was getting rid of her car, and there was no way she'd drive his, so she'd be without transportation.

"You're pushing me to the ends of my limit, Nicole," he said as he stalked toward her.

"Good, then maybe you'll figure it out, and leave me the heck alone," she shouted.

Ryan completely lost his temper. He was standing close to Nicole and lifted his hand quickly in the air in a show of frustration.

Nicole saw his hand rising toward her and terror took over. She cried out with real fear and dropped to the ground, cowering. It had been so many years since she'd been beaten she'd forgotten you couldn't get a man that angry. She rolled up on the ground in a fetal position, her mind flying back to those teenage years when her father had beaten her so badly she'd black out.

Ryan stared in complete shock, his hand still in the air. He looked at Nicole and saw she was terrified. Her expression was haunted, and he knew, beyond a shadow of a doubt, someone had beaten her. They'd not only beaten her, but had done it so badly she was no longer in control of herself from just the thought of him hitting her.

Ryan's temper evaporated instantly, and all he wanted to do was protect her, even if it was from himself. He'd never in his life even thought about hitting a woman, but she didn't know that. He didn't even think she knew exactly who he was at that moment.

"I'm not going to hurt you, Nicole. I don't care how bad we're fighting, or how angry I am. I'd never hurt you. Do you understand?" he asked her softly. She wouldn't look at him. She was in her own world right then. "I'm going to take you upstairs," he told her in the same soft tone. He didn't want to scare her any more than he already had.

He needed answers to what had happened to her. He may have appeared calm on the outside, but inside he was a madman. He wanted to rip the person apart who'd dared to lay a hand on her. Had it been an ex-boyfriend? It was the only answer that made sense to him. How could she have allowed a man to beat her? It had to have happened for quite a long time because terror like that didn't come from a one-time occurrence.

He scooped her into his arms, and she let out a little protest, but then she lay silently against his chest as he carried her up the stairs. He placed her on the bed and went into her bathroom, where he drew a hot bath. He added some different salts and beads, remembering his cousins once said their wives liked to relax with a soothing bubble bath. He figured it would help her, and he was willing to do anything to get that haunted look out of her eyes.

He even lit a few candles, bringing a comforting ambiance. He knew she loved to take candlelit bubble baths and hoped it would help.

Once the tub was ready, he stepped back into the bedroom and found her still lying on the bed.

She looked a bit better, but her face was still white, and he wasn't happy he'd been the one to make her look that way.

"I'm going to undress you now. I have a bath ready for you. I think it will help calm your nerves," he told her, speaking softly. She said nothing as he started pulling her clothes off. He stripped her quickly and, for once, the sight of her body didn't send him over the edge of insanity. He wanted nothing more than to console her.

He carried her into the bathroom, gently lowering her into the tub. She sank into the water, and a sigh escaped her throat. He didn't want to leave her, but he needed some answers, and he was sure he wouldn't get them out of her. He needed to seek out Patsy.

"Will you be okay in here?" he asked her.

"I'm fine, Ryan. I'm sorry about that. I think I'm just tired. I know you'd never hit me," she said, trying to sound casual, but not pulling it off. He bent down and gently took her lips with his, needing to reassure them both that everything was going to be okay.

"I'll be back soon," he told her and walked from the room. He left the door open a crack and told the housekeeper to keep an eye on her. He also had the cook send up something for her to snack on, while she was in the tub. He knew she'd be back to normal soon.

Ryan walked down the hall and knocked on Patsy's door. He was amazed, but a smile came to his face because her music was playing so loud she couldn't have heard anything. He hated to open her door and invade her privacy, but he needed to talk to her. He cracked the door and peeked inside. She was in the middle of the room, dancing around to some obnoxious song coming from the stereo system he'd bought her. At least she appreciated his gifts, he thought.

He smiled, watching her for a few minutes, loving the happy expression on her face. She was a great kid, and he was glad her life was a bit more comfortable than it had been. She swung around and spotted him there, a pink flush coming to her cheeks.

"I didn't hear you come in," she said a bit sheepishly.

"I'm sorry about that. I knocked, but I don't think you would've heard if the house had come falling down around you," he told her a little too loudly, since that was the only way she could hear him.

She walked over to her radio and turned the volume down. There was still a bit of ringing in his ears, and he prayed the horrible song she was listening to didn't get stuck in his head. He thought he really must be getting old because there was a time he would've blasted the radio just as loudly and danced along with her.

"What's up, Ryan?"

"I was wondering if we could talk for a few minutes. Can you come downstairs with me?" he asked. He didn't want to get lost in her chaotic room. She was certainly not a clean freak, but what teenager was?

"Sure, I was starting to crave some chocolate, anyway," she agreed and followed him to the kitchen. He waited while she grabbed some brownies and milk and sat at the table with him. The cook had long ago discovered her love of brownies and always made sure to have fresh ones

213

ready daily. The entire staff had fallen in love with both Patsy and Nicole.

"I want to talk to you about Nicole. She won't want to talk to me about it, but I need to know so that I can help her," he said to Patsy, making sure she was looking at him and could understand what he was saying.

"You want to know about the beatings, don't you?" she asked him, completely shocking him. She said it in almost a casual tone, but he could see the pain behind her eyes.

"Yes," he said. He didn't know what else he could say, so he sat back and waited for her to speak. She looked at her plate, and then pushed it away as if she'd lost her appetite. He could relate to that. He didn't think he'd be able to ever eat again.

"It started when she was still pretty young," Patsy began, and he was shocked. Who the hell would've beaten her when she was young? He simply couldn't comprehend what she was telling him. "When Dad lost his job, he sank to an all-time low. He was always grouchy and kind of cruel with his words, but when he lost work, he started taking it out on Nicole. Mom was a drunk and didn't help at home. As I got older, he started noticing me more, but Nicole always got between us. She never once allowed him to hit me, but that just meant she took twice as much. I know he cracked a few of her bones, and she was always black and blue," she said as a tear tracked down her cheek.

"He was really careful to never hit her in the face, though. He couldn't let anyone see how he was terrorizing her. I begged for her to let me tell someone, but she said she'd take it until she turned eighteen. Then she'd be able to look after me. She said, if we ever told anyone, they'd put us in foster care, and we wouldn't be in the same home. She was always so strong too. She never screamed, or even cried out. Her tears would fall, which that bastard seemed to really enjoy. It seemed his whole purpose in life was to break her, but she was so strong. He never really did break her. I think she hurt far more when you were no longer a part of her life than when he hit her," Patsy finished. Tears were now soaking her face, and he handed her napkins.

"I never knew," he said painfully.

"Nobody knew because that's how she wanted it. When we left, neither of us ever looked back. When they died, neither of us cried. We didn't feel any loss. To tell you the truth, we both felt safer knowing there was no chance he could come after us again. If it wouldn't have been for Nicole, he would've broken me. I'm not nearly as strong as her, and I couldn't have taken the beatings like she did. I tried though, Ryan. I really did. I tried to come between them, but she'd lock me out of her room, and I'd hear him through the doorway, hitting her over and over again," she said, openly sobbing. She couldn't talk anymore.

Ryan pulled her onto his lap and rubbed her back, trying to comfort her the best way he knew how. His gut hurt so much, he didn't know how he wasn't throwing up. He couldn't believe he'd never known what she'd gone through. It was beyond a nightmare, and he'd done nothing in the last several months except to terrify her more. He felt like the lowest human being on the earth.

She must hate him, and God help him, but he still couldn't set her free. He was certainly going to change a few things, but he needed her in his life. He needed to see her when he walked in the door. He needed to hear her voice ringing out through the hallways, and he needed to smell her sweet scent. He couldn't free her, but he knew she might leave eventually. She'd already been through hell and didn't need to live it for the rest of her life.

He rocked Patsy in his arms while she sobbed out her own pain. He couldn't imagine the terror she'd gone through herself. She'd only been a toddler when all that had occurred. He guessed the fates had stepped in to save them both. He wished her father was still alive because he'd never wanted to seriously harm someone as badly as he wanted to at that moment.

"I'm okay now," Patsy gulped, as she looked at him with her innocent eyes. She seemed more like twelve than sixteen.

"I'm sorry you went through all that and I'm even sorrier I wasn't there for you," he told her, fighting to not show his own pain.

"You couldn't have been there for us. She didn't allow anyone to help her shoulder the pain,"

217

Patsy told him. He knew she was right, but it sure didn't make him feel any better. When she'd sent him walking, he'd never looked back. He hadn't wanted to show her any weakness and, because of that, she'd been hurt.

He swore to make it up to her. He'd make sure her life was so much better than it had ever been before. She'd never have to worry about money or where she was going to sleep. He smiled wryly at himself, thinking about how well that conversation would go over.

He'd make sure she and her sister were okay, and her love of Patsy is what he'd use to get her to accept his offering. He knew she'd already gone to the ends of the earth for her sister, and he also knew she'd continue to do so for the rest of her life.

Her sacrifices weren't even sacrifices in her own eyes. She believed everyone would do the same thing for their family. She was so wrong. Most people he'd ever known didn't give a lick about anyone or anything but themselves. She was an exception.

Patsy finally pulled herself together, and he went back into the den to have another drink. He had to calm down again before he saw her. Patsy had promised not to tell Nicole of their conversation. He hated to have Nicole's sister keep secrets from her, but he also didn't want her on the defensive because he knew her secrets. He had to be careful not to act too differently around her, or she'd be furious. She obviously didn't want to be pitied, and she didn't want to be a martyr.

He finally had himself under control enough to walk up the stairs. He'd been gone over an hour and was shocked to find her still in the tub. She was lying back in the water, but she was awake. He walked in and groaned, as the bubbles were quickly fading. He reached in and felt the water had cooled off, so he turned the faucet on hot to re-warm the tub.

"I can do that myself," she said, bringing her knees up to her chest in modesty. He looked at her with his brows raised high. She was hiding not only what he'd seen many times over but licked, sucked and done just about everything imaginable to. As if she could read his thoughts, her cheeks turned scarlet, and she quickly looked away.

He released some of the cooler water, and soon the tub was back up to a nice temperature and full of new bubbles. She relaxed her body, eyeing him warily. He blew out his breath, reminding himself to not act differently. What would he have done before his world had been knocked off of its axis? That was easy. He would've joined her in the tub.

He gave her a very seductive smile and began stripping his clothing off. She looked at him in shock, and he could see she was trying to decide whether to stay in the safety of her bubbles, or to jump out of the tub. He really hoped she'd stayed.

He got his clothes off, not even trying to hide his desire for her, and stepped into the tub. He moved her forward and sat down behind her, quickly pulling her into his arms. It was like coming home. She leaned against him tensely for a few moments, and when he didn't try doing anything other than hold her, she finally started to relax.

"I didn't want to go to that party, anyway," he said, as if not attending was his idea.

"Ha," she said, with a jerk of her shoulder. He had to fight off the smile. He loved how she had to have the last word, and he loved how he could wipe all words from her. He began rubbing his hands against her stomach. He felt the shudder run through her body, and his worries started melting away.

His hands soon traveled up her soapy body until they gripped her incredibly luscious breasts. He rubbed her hardened nipples between his fingers, causing her to gasp out loud. He was beyond aroused at that point and couldn't imagine a time when she wouldn't turn his brain to mush.

His hands kept stroking her, making moans of pleasure escape her body. He wanted her supple and willing to concede to his every wish before he started the conversation he wanted to have with her. It was really hard to use sex as a way to get what he wanted, though, because the second he touched her, his own mind went out the window, and he tended to forget what he wanted to talk about.

She pushed her body back against him, and he was the one who let a moan escape. She was slippery and wet, and he was beyond ready to join their bodies together. He leaned forward and kissed along her slender neck, nipping and licking the tender skin. He loved the taste and smell of her. His one hand continued to massage her breast, while his other hand slipped lower on her body, finding her aching nub and making her cry out in pleasure. It didn't take him long, rubbing her swollen womanhood, before she began shaking in pleasure.

He slid his fingers inside her moist heat and felt her contractions grip him as she flew over the edge in ecstasy. She was so responsive to his every touch he should've known he never could count on having a conversation in the middle of love-making.

He quickly turned her body around, so she was straddling him, and took her ripe nipple into his mouth. He had to taste her skin. He had to feel her heartbeat against him. He had to have her right then.

He lifted her hips above his straining erection and slowly lowered her on his shaft. He groaned as her heat surrounded him. She was so tight, wet, and hot he couldn't hold off. She took over for him and braced her hands on his shoulders, moving her hips up and down on his thick shaft.

He grabbed her head, bringing it down to his, needing to drink from her lips. He thrust his tongue inside her soft mouth, tasting her and tangling their tongues together. He held her back so she was smashed up against him. Her breasts were rubbing against his chest, causing lightning to shoot down his entire body. She moved her hips faster and faster, up and down his throbbing shaft. He could feel her body getting even tighter as she neared orgasm again. She was so unbelievably responsive.

He couldn't tear his lips away from hers. He kept greedily drinking as she kept up the intense rhythm of their love-making.

Suddenly, she ripped her head away and cried out as her body grabbed him so tightly, it was almost painful for him. She was gripping him over and over again with the strength of her release,

223

sending him spiraling out of control. He moved his hands down to grip her hips as he surged into her as far as he could go and shot his release deep within her. He could feel himself pumping repeatedly, giving her every single ounce of himself.

The orgasm was so powerful, it felt as if a piece of his soul had departed him and seeped into her. She truly owned him, if only she knew. There was nothing in the world he wouldn't do for her. He prayed she never knew that because it might end up destroying him, if the one thing she asked for was to be set free.

He pulled her head down to his shoulder, not wanting her to see into his eyes but needing her to be next to him. He needed them to be skin to skin with his body inside her, never moving from that position. He stroked her back as they both enjoyed the aftermath. Neither of them was willing to speak or break the moment. Their conversation would have to wait until later.

CHAPTER TEN

"Fine. I'll use the stupid car then," Nicole said as she threw her hands up in frustration. She'd called a cab to pick her up and take her to work, and when Ryan found out, he flipped.

Ryan had sent one of his security men to the gate to pay the driver and send him on his way. There was no way in hell he was letting her call a cab when she had a vehicle to drive.

He'd blocked her entrance at the front door and wasn't moving an inch on the matter. If she wanted to leave the house, it was going to be in the car he'd bought her. He stood there, blocking the door, with the keys dangling from his fingers and a smug look on his face. She'd finally backed down and let him have his way.

"Was that really so hard?" He practically growled at her.

"Yes, it was, and thanks for asking," she mocked him. He wanted to bend her over his knee. Of course, that thought got his mind going in the wrong direction, and he was already late for a board meeting. He had to hurry and get his work finished at the office so he could get over to the shop and meet the architect for the remodel work Jasmine had requested. He found it amusing. He'd much rather be doing that than sitting in his office.

Nicole didn't know he'd be at her work place later that day, and he was looking forward to surprising her. He didn't think it was going to be a surprise she was delighted about, but that was just too bad for her.

Nicole grabbed the keys from him with a little huff and marched out to the garage with him right on her heels. He loved watching the sway of her

226

hips as she walked away from him, especially when she was in a tiff and the movements were more pronounced.

"Are you stalking me now?" she asked as she stepped through the garage door.

"I'm leaving for work, too," he informed her and chuckled. That earned him another glare.

"Well, then, I'll see you later," she said and reached for her car door. He spun her around and kissed her long and hard, leaving her breathless.

"Think about that today," he said, and then jumped in his car and drove away.

Nicole stood there dazed for a few moments and blew out her breath in frustration. The man got under her skin in seconds. He evoked powerful emotions in her--whether it was anger, lust, or happiness. He didn't do anything halfway.

She pulled onto the street and had to stop a couple miles down the road at a drugstore. She'd put off taking a pregnancy test for a ridiculous amount of time and knew it was time. She was terrified to confirm what she already knew in her heart, but she had to do it. She wouldn't take the test at home where Ryan could read her face like a book.

She walked out of the store with the test safely stored in her handbag and had to control her breathing. What scared her more than knowing the truth was how much she wanted the baby. At first she'd been terrified to think she was pregnant, and then as the thought had sunk in that she was most likely carrying Ryan's baby, she'd been overwhelmed with joy.

She knew, beyond a shadow of a doubt, her love for Ryan had never gone away. She'd loved him with the innocence of a child and, since living with him, that love had grown into an adult's deep and binding love. She knew he didn't love her, and that knowledge was enough to destroy her.

She knew he desired her and, in the months they'd been together, that desire had turned into a red hot inferno. It seemed neither of them could get enough of each other, but that wasn't enough to make a relationship work, especially with a baby on the way. She had such mixed feelings over the test. She wanted the baby with an overwhelming desire but, at the same time, she was terrified of what that would mean between Ryan and her.

She walked into the shop and, for once, was grateful neither Jasmine nor Trinity was there. They were as bad as Ryan at reading her every expression, and she really needed time to take her test and deal with the emotions to follow, whether the answer was yes or no.

She couldn't wait even a second longer and headed straight for the bathroom. Shakily, she read the instructions. Then she sat with the small stick sitting on the edge of the sink. She waited a full ten minutes before getting the courage to grab the stick again and see what the results were.

Her eyes filled with tears and overflowed down her cheeks, but they were not tears of sadness, or even terror. They were tears of complete joy. She'd already known the answer, so she really didn't see why the stick turning blue should be able to fill her with so much emotion, but it was a confirmation that she was carrying Ryan's baby within her womb.

By the size of her stomach, she figured she was several months along already too. She was surprised he hadn't said anything about her weight gain. Actually, looking back, he'd made a comment she was so much healthier, and that her body was even more attractive to him. She smiled as she thought how his tune would change when she was as big as a whale.

She wasn't ready to share her secret with anyone yet, so she stayed in the bathroom a while longer. She had to get control over her features, or the girls would know for sure something was up. She buried the test at the bottom of the garbage can and walked out.

Jasmine had arrived but was literally buried to her elbows in batter, so she couldn't follow Nicole around, as she sometimes did. Trinity ended up calling them and saying she couldn't make it in because her youngest child had a cold. Nicole knew the women loved owning their own place-- most of all because it allowed them to be mothers first.

She unconsciously rubbed her hand along her stomach and thought she'd love to be a full-time mother. If she could still work for them, she'd get to make that a reality. The place was set up for kids, with a nursery in the back and a playground out front. It would be ideal for a new mother.

She had real hope, and she wanted to shout to the world she was going to be a mother. It would be hard not to say anything to Ryan that night, but she wasn't sure if she wanted to share with him yet. She didn't know how he was going to react to the news. She knew he loved children because he was amazing with his cousins' kids, but he'd been emphatic with her that their relationship was a temporary thing.

A child tied them together unlike anything else, and even when they went their separate ways, they would always be a part of each other's lives. It was all too complicated, so she decided to make some floral arrangements to get her mind off the situation.

"Good morning," Ryan said, getting Nicole's attention. She jerked in surprise and looked up with guilty eyes.

Ryan wondered what she was up to. He'd stood there watching her for several minutes, and she'd been concentrating so hard on what she was doing she hadn't been aware of anything around her.

"What are you doing here?" she asked him suspiciously.

"I'm meeting an architect here for the girls. They want some remodel work done," he told her.

"Oh, I didn't know," she said, seeming to breathe a relieved sigh. She really had his curiosity up. She wasn't normally one to keep secrets. If she wanted to say something, she outright said it, and to hell with the consequences.

"It looks like we'll be around each other a lot because this project will take at least a couple months," he said with a self-satisfied smile.

Her eyes rounded at his words, and he enjoyed the look of surprise on her face.

"Well, um…I need to do some stuff in the back," she said and then ran away. He was close to chasing her down and demanding to know why she was acting odd, but the man he was meeting showed up, and that kept him busy for several hours.

By the time he was finished, Nicole managed to pull herself together, and he knew he was getting nothing out of her. Ryan had discovered, over the last several months, that even though she infuriated him on a continual basis, he couldn't imagine living without her — or Patsy, for that matter.

He looked forward to seeing them both when he walked in the door, and his once empty home was filled with warmth and laughter. He didn't want that to go away. Now that he knew what she'd gone through as a child, he knew she hadn't left him for the reasons he'd once thought. It was time to put his heart out on the table and take a gamble.

He was afraid, if she rejected him again, he'd never be the same, but he didn't want to continue on the way things had been. He didn't want her to give him everything of herself in their bed and nothing in the daylight.

"I have to head back home. I'll see you in a few hours," he said. Taking her in his arms, he kissed her with so much tenderness it left tears in her eyes. Nicole stared at him with a shell-shocked expression and simply nodded at him.

Ryan walked out of the shop, whistling and feeling positive about the night to come. He went home and began setting the scene for what he hoped would be a romantic night with a very happy ending.

###

Nicole got held up at the shop. The girls never asked her to stay late, but they'd needed inventory done and asked for her help. It was eight by the time she made her way out the door. She was dead on her feet and still in shock over the pregnancy test.

She'd figured out she'd simply tell him the truth and explain a baby didn't mean they needed to change things. They could come to a mutual agreement so they could both be equal participants in their child's life. She hated the thought of them being nothing more than strangers. It hurt her in ways nothing had ever hurt before.

Nicole stepped into the house and looked around in confusion. The lighting was incredibly dim, and no one seemed to be about. She looked down at the floor and saw rose petals everywhere. Had someone spilled something? Had there been an accident? She followed the path and found herself in the dining room.

Nicole gasped as she saw the scene before her. Her body began to tremble, and her mind refused to acknowledge what she was seeing. Ryan was standing at one end of the room in a tuxedo, which showed his impressive body off to perfection. The man really wore a tux well, she thought. He was stunning, and she could barely pull her eyes away from his magnificent form.

She looked at the table that was set for seduction. There were candles burning and more rose petals strewn about. Champagne was chilling, and the aromas drifting in the air made her stomach growl in hunger. In the middle of it all, there was the largest rose bouquet she'd ever seen. A romantic song was playing in the background, causing her body to react.

"What is all this?" she asked in awe.

"I thought you deserved a bit of romance," he told her, passion burning in his eyes. It took her breath away. He'd gone to so much trouble.

"I . . . I don't know what to say," she finally gasped. She felt the prickle of tears come to her eyes and quickly turned, not wanting him to see. She blamed her weak emotions on her pregnancy.

"Dance with me," he gently commanded, and then she was in his arms. She didn't even think about resisting him. She fit into his arms as if they were meant to be together. She laid her head on his masculine shoulder, and he pulled her tightly against his hard body.

He smelled like home, and she burrowed even closer against him. She didn't care about anything other than that moment. She needed to have this night with him before she told him about the baby and their world changed. She knew she'd look back on their night together, and it would cause pain, but at least she'd be able to honestly tell her child how much she was in love with her father.

Nicole had the feeling she'd still be in love with him until the day she died. She'd never loved another, and something like that didn't just fall away. She'd certainly lose a piece of her soul when he ended their relationship.

Ryan spun her around the room in a gentle dance that was for just the two of them. He bent his head down and took her lips with his in such tender passion her heart grew to twice its normal size. She ran her hands up his neck and pulled him even closer.

He broke apart from her and took a step back, leaving her unsure and aching. He never broke contact with her, and she didn't think that was a good sign. She didn't know it, but she was looking at him with her heart in her eyes, and she'd given herself away.

Ryan gritted his teeth. "I want you badly. Never doubt that, but tonight is about romance, and if I keep kissing you, dinner will be forgotten, and we'll end up in bed," he growled at her. Her chest puffed up with pride. She knew it was only sex, but weren't many other relationships built on so much less than that?

Ryan sat her down at the table and, within moments, a plate was set before her. They ate their meal, and she found herself relaxing. He'd gone to a lot of trouble to give her a romantic night, and she was feeling the effects of it. He poured her a glass of champagne, and she didn't say anything. She just made sure she didn't pick it up instead of her water.

Over their dessert, Ryan took her hand in his and started caressing her wrist, which immediately sent her pulse skyrocketing. She didn't think she'd ever get enough of him.

"Nicole, you're unlike any other woman I've ever known and--before you get all defensive-- that's a good thing. You're beautiful, without a doubt, but you're also compassionate, loyal, giving, passionate, stubborn and everything else any man could possibly ever want. I started this relationship wanting to punish you for leaving me.

No — don't try and pull away — let me finish,"
he said when she tried removing her hands.

She squirmed in her seat but stopped trying to
pull away. She could hear him out, but it sounded
as if he was about to break up with her, and she
didn't know how she was going to listen to him
with her heart breaking apart. She wanted to rub
her stomach and somehow guard her unborn child
from hearing his words.

"I'm trying to say I screwed up. I tried to
punish you for leaving me, but I know what really
happened. Patsy talked to me, and I wish so much
you would've told me. I would have been there for
you and protected you. I loved you then, and I
love you now, and it nearly destroys me to know I
wasn't there to keep you safe. I should've been the
one taking your pain. I should've known
something was wrong, but I let pride get in my
way. I'll never let that happen again. I'm laying
my heart before you — right here and now. I love
you, Nicole, and I can't imagine my life without
you in it. Please accept my love, and let me protect
you for the rest of my life," he said tenderly, never
breaking eye-contact.

Nicole couldn't even breathe as tears trailed down her cheeks. She'd thought he was breaking up with her. Instead, he was giving her his love. She didn't see how she deserved such an amazing man. She hated him knowing about the abuse. It made her feel weak, but as she looked into his eyes, she realized he didn't think of her as weak at all. She believed he really did love her. She stared at him in wonder.

Her hand drifted up to his face. He said nothing else. He simply held her hand and waited for her to get her emotions under control. She stared into his eyes, looking for anything there that might belie his words. She saw nothing but love and acceptance within their depths.

"I love you too, Ryan. I always have, and I had to send you away back then because I didn't want you to know how weak I was," she began.

"Don't you dare ever say you were weak. You're the strongest person I've ever known, and you took all that punishment for your sister's sake. You took the weight of the world on your shoulders, you stubborn fool. I would've gladly taken that weight for you, but I understand why you did it. Now you have me by your side, and we can conquer anything as long as we're together," he interrupted her.

"I was a fool, Ryan. I always blamed myself for the beatings, and I thought you would be horrified and leave me anyway if you knew about it. I was so young," she said in explanation.

"Tell me again," he demanded, and she knew what he wanted to hear.

"I love you, Ryan Titan. I always have, and I always will, even when you're driving me insane with your caveman ways," she said with true joy in her voice. She knew they'd be fine. She knew her life would be okay from that day forward. He crushed her lips beneath his before she could tell him about the baby.

It was several minutes before they broke apart for air, and she was left even more breathless by the pure love shining through his eyes. He suddenly let go of her and dropped to his knee. She gasped in shock, and more tears tracked down her face.

"Marry me, Nicole. Make an honest man out of me. Always tell me when I'm wrong, love me day and night, give me children, and let me help you fulfill all your dreams," he said with a choked up voice. She sobbed as she shook her head yes. She couldn't have gotten words past her throat if her life depended on it.

He opened the small velvet box, and she was surprised she didn't faint. He was presenting her an exquisite diamond ring. The center stone was perfect, surrounded by a beautiful pattern of smaller diamonds. She watched him take it from the box and slip it on her finger. She stared down at the sparkling ring, a symbol of his love.

"I hope you like it. I had it made especially for you," he said, sounding unsure.

"It's stunning, Ryan, but you didn't have to get such a large one. I would've been happy with a simple band," she told him, meaning what she said.

He looked at her as if she was insane."If your ring size equaled the love I feel for you, you wouldn't be able to lift your hand. I actually toned it down a bit from what I originally wanted," he said a bit sheepishly. She threw her arms around his neck and held on tightly. How could she have ever taken his generosity as controlling?

He'd been showing her love all along, just in the wrong ways. He'd bought her things, which she'd continued to reject, because it was the only way he knew how to show love. She'd teach him what she really wanted, and that was only him.

"So you want a lot of children, huh?" she asked him slyly.

"I'd love to fill this house from top to bottom with them," he said with a wicked smile.

"I don't know about filling the place from top to bottom, but I could manage to have one in here in about five months," she said and waited for it to sink in. She watched as his eyes looked at her in confusion for a few moments and then widened as what she said dawned on him.

He looked from her eyes to her stomach and back up again, and she nodded at him. His mouth parted in the biggest smile she'd ever seen him give, and he grabbed the hem of her shirt and lifted it out of his way. He ran his hand over her stomach, which was just barely beginning to show.

"How could I not have realized?" he asked her, as his hand continued to caress the smooth surface. His rubbing wasn't meant to be sexual, but he was turning her body to liquid fire with his innocent caress.

"I've suspected for a while but just found out for sure today. At first, I thought I was getting fat from all the food you've been feeding me," she said a bit sheepishly.

"I love your body. Don't ever say anything like that again. I've enjoyed your curves and was simply so turned on by you I didn't pay attention to the changes," he said with real passion behind his words.

"Ryan, you're so good for me."

"I plan on being there for you every day for the rest of our lives," he told her. He took her back into his arms, and the talking came to an end. He carried her to their room, where he worshiped her body, noticing the slight changes his child was causing in her and became even more turned on than ever before, knowing they'd created a life together.

They stayed up late into the night, lovemaking, talking and planning for their future together, both of them feeling a peace unlike anything either of them had ever known.

EPILOGUE

"Blow out the candles, baby," Nicole said to her two-year-old daughter. She couldn't believe how much her life had changed in the last few years. She was happier than she could've ever thought possible.

The crowd erupted in applause as Jordin blew out her two candles and rewarded everyone with her precious smile and giggles.

"That's Daddy's good girl. I can't believe how big you are," Ryan said to his daughter before scooping her up in his arms.

He then wrapped Nicole close, still as passionate about her as the day they'd reunited. He couldn't seem to get enough of her. She'd given him the gift of his daughter, and her love, and he couldn't be any happier.

He looked around his yard, grateful for the beautiful Seattle day. There wasn't a cloud in the sky, as if the fates were shining down on them. His cousins were playing on the enormous play structure with their children. He smiled at his ever-growing family.

He laughed to himself, thinking how hard he and his cousins had fought marriage and commitments. None of them could picture their lives without their beautiful brides, and to top it off, the women all got along so amazingly well together. They'd quickly become best friends, sharing their shop, and motherhood, with each other.

They were all a family, closer than anyone he knew. Jasmine called Nicole over, and he reluctantly let her go and watched as she laughed with the other two women. He headed over to the play structure, where Jordin squirmed to get down and play with her cousins.

"We've done really well, cousin," Drew said with a satisfied smile as his focus ran from his children to his wife.

"Yes we have," Ryan agreed triumphantly.

"I can't believe how stupid we were to think life was complete without these women in it," Derek added. The three men all nodded together.

"I feel like the luckiest man alive. I have an amazing wife, beautiful daughter, and though Nicole wanted to wait a couple more weeks to tell you, I can't stand not sharing. She's pregnant again," he told them.

"That's wonderful," Drew said, slapping Ryan's back hard enough to send a lesser man to his knees.

"Congratulations," Derek added with enthusiasm.

"How is Patsy doing?" Drew asked.

"She's loving college, but man do I miss her. I'm glad she decided to stay closer to home, but still, we don't see her enough with her living on campus. I've already had to scare the crap out of one guy who was getting far too amorous with her. She was mad at me for weeks because he won't even look at her now," Ryan said with satisfaction.

"I would've done the same thing. I can't even imagine what I'm going to go through when my kids begin to date," Derek said with a narrowing of his eyes.

"Yeah, I know. Patsy is technically my sister-in-law, but I think of her like a daughter, and I swear I'll destroy any guy who tries to hurt her," he told them.

"I almost feel sorry for the poor guys who try and over-step their bounds," Derek said, but the look in his eyes contradicted his words. He'd thoroughly enjoy terrorizing those men.

"At least we have a long time to prepare," Ryan said.

"Amen," both of his cousins agreed.

"Come eat, boys," Trinity called, and the men eagerly headed to their wives. Nothing gave any of them greater joy than time spent with family. They'd been wealthy, but marriage and children made them richer than kings, and they counted their blessings daily.

The Tycoon Series Continues with;

The Tycoon's Secret

Made in the USA
Las Vegas, NV
26 June 2023